Forget Me Not

D1343016

MARIE SIBBONS

Prologue

The narrow stairs creaked at every third step taken as if it were telling her to turn around. Despite knowing she was alone in the house, she winced at each sound made as she climbed towards the attic room. Ahead of her, white and silvery clouds were lending a shimmering glow to the otherwise dark room. Her reflection appeared in the cracked windowpane as she took the final step onto the ragged carpet. Taking off her glasses as she moved closer to the image, she could see the blotches under both tired red eyes. They reminded her of the disappointment she had experienced a few hours earlier before the wine had temporarily washed away the tears.

And yet the day had started so hopefully. Maybe it wasn't over yet. Maybe, just maybe… No, she thought to herself, it is over, and she must accept it.

Crouching to open the tiny cupboard door, she looked down and noticed a teardrop splashing onto the wooden box still in her hands. It was a box she had no place opening. She recalled her conversation with that old woman in the nursing home which had made her feel so ashamed. It was time to move on with her own life, not dwell on someone else's past. Tomorrow would be a new day, different from all the others.

She placed the box inside the cupboard and closed the door for the last time.

Then she heard the stairs creak.

Part One

Chapter One

4th January 1995

Christine shuffled her feet to keep warm as she stood shivering in the doorway. She knew this was the right house. It was the only one in the row without an impressive flower display in the front garden, a sure sign that it was not owner-occupied. Come on Judy, she thought impatiently, you must know I'm coming today.

It had been a long journey from her parent's home in France to the cottage door and Christine was tired, cold, and irritable. She knocked for the fourth time then shouted 'hello' through the cast iron letterbox, her fingers jamming for the second time. Judy had to be in. It wasn't as if she had anywhere else to be.

Finally, there was some movement behind the obscure glass in the door, a key turning, and then, a young male face, devoid of expression, looking back at her. He said nothing to Christine, just yawned. Christine was not surprised or embarrassed at the dishevelled state of the young man. She had enough experience in house sharing with men.

'Oh, hi. I'm Christine. Is Judy there? I'm moving in today too. Has she told you about me? Nothing too bad, I hope.'

The young man opened the door a few inches more, revealing a blue mohair dressing gown, its belt hanging precariously from a single loop. Christine smiled awkwardly and glanced down at her rucksack, telling herself he was probably just about to have a shower. The door stayed where it was, but the young man stepped aside, clutching the two sides of his dressing-gown to protect his dignity. Christine grabbed the rucksack and stepped into the cottage while there was a gap.

'I guess you live here too,' she said cheerily, trying to get some verbal interaction while looking around the hallway.

The young man yawned once more but finally engaged in the conversation. 'So, it would seem. Here's a key. Your rooms are at the front end with adjacent doors. Mine's at the back,' he replied, with a continued lack of interest.

'Oh,' she said quickly, before he switched off once again. 'It's just me moving in today. Judy moved in New Year's Day.'

He slowly walked back up the carpeted staircase before stopping. 'You're half right. It's just you,' he quipped, not even turning around.

Christine pushed a half-open door and walked into a cottage-style sitting room. Although not sure she would have chosen such an old-fashioned house, it was certainly an improvement on the last one. The two-seater sofa looked just as old as the one in their last house, yet it had been upholstered and didn't sink to the floor when she sat down on it. She pictured herself and Judy sitting close together watching television. It would be easier now she was single once again. She knew that Judy had felt uncomfortable being in the same room as her and Gary even though he barely noticed her. Well, now it would just be the two of them again, and, of course, that barrel of laughs upstairs and he looked as if he spent most of his spare time in bed.

A local newspaper lay on the cushion next to her and, glancing at the headline, she shuddered.

A THIRD WOMAN ATTACKED IN SHOREDITCH

Crikey! That was another reason not to fall out again, she thought, picturing the lonely bus stop where she worked. Maybe she should offer Judy petrol money for all those lifts to and from work.

Over the Christmas holiday, Christine had relived the past few weeks with Judy in her mind. The fact that this was their third place together proved that they had a connection of some sort. She remembered how they had bonded during the summer TEFL course they both enrolled in last year, sharing horror stories of disastrous lessons, dissatisfied students, and soul-destroying feedback from their tutors. The two women had hit it off immediately and Christine had jumped at the opportunity to move into Judy's rented house. For a while, they enjoyed each other's company and would happily spend their free time together despite living and working in the same place. But that was only for a while.

It wasn't clear when or why they had fallen out to such an extent. Christine supposed they were probably both at fault. Before she returned from France, she had resolved to be more understanding towards Judy's peculiar ways, idiosyncrasies that would drive most sane people to despair. There were selfish reasons too. This new house was nowhere near the bus station, so getting to work without a car would be extremely difficult. Also, Christine's other friends seemed to be drifting away from her. Emma and Tim had moved in together and the others hadn't asked Christine if she wanted the vacant room. So, here she was once again renting with Judy but this time they would only have each other for company.

Forgetting the departing words of the young man in his dressing gown, she climbed the stairs to inspect her bedroom, but on entering the first bedroom she began to have an inkling that something had not gone to plan. The room was empty save for the requisite furniture: a wardrobe, a desk, and a single bed. No sign of hers or Judy's belongings. Were they still in the other house? Even a couple of days was plenty of time for squatters to move into the old house. She began to imagine her New Year's resolution to get on better with Judy becoming a distant memory, until she went into the second bedroom. That too was empty of personal possessions, and, for the first time, she realized that Judy hadn't moved in.

It's just you. Now the words hit home. Somehow, she had arrived at the new house before Judy. Where on earth was she? A knock at the front door drew Christine back downstairs in the expectation that her question would be answered. But it wasn't to be.

The landlord of the property greeted Christine as he brushed past her, uninvited, into the sitting room. He was a well-spoken, middle-aged man, confident in manner, friendly but clearly in a hurry as he was still holding an outwardly pointing car key. He had bad news for Christine.

'I'm afraid I have had to let both rooms to someone else. Your friend promised to sign the contract and pay the deposit by January 3rd, but I haven't heard from her since she viewed the house two weeks ago. I cannot afford to leave the rooms empty any longer. It's not fair on Dane either as he would be stuck paying the bills himself. I take it your friend changed her mind and decided to stay where she was.'

Christine, embarrassed to be standing inside a house she had no right to be in, was annoyed: annoyed at Judy for not telling her of the change of plan, and at the landlord for not caring she had no place to live. But she left without protest. At least she wouldn't have to share a house with Dane!

There was no problem going back to the old house that she had been so relieved to leave almost three weeks earlier. She still had her key, and her things were sure to still be there given that Judy had not moved them. Christine's heart sank as she glanced up at the scruffy old house standing out from the other houses in the short terrace by virtue of the tiny dormer in its roof. The curtains in the bottom bay window hung unevenly, half-drawn, exposing an upright mattress. Clearly, no one had taken that room during her absence. But why would they have? She and Judy had been the only occupants for months. No one else had even viewed the many vacant rooms while they lived there.

Once inside, she looked down the dim hallway and saw Russell emptying the cupboards in the kitchen. He was a former tenant who moved out just after they had moved in. He still collected the rent for the landlord, although he appeared to be doing more than that right at that moment. Recognizing her ground coffee and Jacob's cream crackers sticking out of a cardboard box on the floor, she marched towards him.

'What are you doing with my food?'

Russell jumped and turned around to see her near-black eyes glaring at him. He squinted his eyes to focus on Christine who, with her slim figure and short dark hair, could resemble a teenage boy from a distance. In stark contrast, he wore his long blond hair tied back in a ponytail, and, with his long eyelashes, cornflower blue eyes, and cupid's bow mouth, could be described as effeminate if it wasn't for his grunge style tattered clothes. When he realized it was her, he dropped a packet of dried pasta on the work top.

'I thought you had left,' he replied, with no apology, 'so I was chucking out any food left in the cupboards in case of mice. You know these houses are teeming with them, right?'

With a shudder, Christine rushed over to where he was standing and took her food out of the box and put it back in the cupboard. 'How would I know when you didn't tell us about them before we moved in? Of course, that was before you moved out,' she added sarcastically.

If she thought he would be embarrassed, she was wrong. She wondered if he was even listening to her, his body language suggesting otherwise.

'Where's Judy?' she asked him.

The question seemed to grab his attention as he looked at her quizzically. 'How should I know? She left over a week ago. Didn't she tell you where she was going?'

'But she must be here. She never moved into the other house, so she has obviously changed her mind about moving out.'

Christine wondered if Russell was lying to cover up for being caught stealing her food, though she doubted he would go to so much effort.

'Well, she isn't,' he replied. 'Have a look in her room. All her stuff has gone, except a pair of glasses.'

'Her glasses! She can't drive without them.'

'To be honest, the bin is the best place for the glasses she left behind. Your room has still got black bags in it. I was about to chuck them too so it's just as well you showed up when you did. She mentioned that she might look for somewhere else just for a couple of weeks as she didn't like being here alone, so she must have found somewhere. She even left her key behind, though she still owes a week's rent. Sorry, but you are the only one here now.'

Christine was puzzled. She knew that Judy was scared about staying in the house by herself but surely she would have let her know if she had moved to a different place. And even if she had moved somewhere temporarily, where was she right now? Besides, she couldn't exactly disappear with Christine's deposit - the deposit she had scraped together before she left so Judy would include her in any move. Both women worked in the same college so were certain to see each other again.

Even more than taking her deposit, Christine couldn't imagine Judy leaving without paying any rent that she owed. If she had any qualities, honesty was certainly one of them. It was as if she had an invisible watcher placing her good and bad deeds into a pair of scales to decide whether she'd passed the test of life. On the other hand, Judy was not blessed with good organizational skills and now Christine was stuck here without the means to go anywhere else. She was on her own, just like Russell said.

After Russell had left, she checked every room from the attic down, checking behind curtains, and under beds for a note that Judy may have left in the wrong place. It was useless. Judy had gone and did not want Christine to follow her. Yet Christine thought they had agreed everything before leaving. She locked the front door before making herself a black coffee and thinking about when they had first moved into the house. They were still speaking then. Or were they? She couldn't quite remember.

What was certain was their friendship had been pushed to the brink during the few months they lived there.

Chapter Two

Three months earlier.

The two women drove up and down the ramshackle Victorian terrace for the third time.

'Which one is it? There are no numbers on any of the doors.'

'It'll be the one that looks lived in, of course, Christine.'

'Judy, none of them look lived in.'

A shift of light behind a textured glass door drew the women's attention to the middle house.

'At least there's plenty of parking,' Judy quipped, as she switched off the engine.

'That would explain why there is not another living soul in sight. Oh well. I suppose this is our last hope.'

The first thing they noticed was the mattresses in the hallway. Leaning against the staircase, their battered lumpy condition was not a good sign of things to come. The young man showing them around saw the focus of their eyes.

'Handy for friends staying over – the odd night of course.'

The two women looked at each other then back at the young man.

'I doubt we'll need them,' replied Judy, unimpressed.

'You speak only for yourself Judy,' retorted Christine. 'I have a thousand friends.'

Don't include me amongst them, thought Judy.

'Russell, is that a French accent I hear?'

A young woman appeared from behind an old wooden door, bringing with her a faint odour of Chinese food.

'Bien sur.'

Judy gave an imaginary eyeroll. Why were people so interested in Christine just because she was French? London was filled with foreign people.

'So, are you sharing?' asked the young man.

'No,' the women said in unison though Christine appeared the more insulted of the two.

'We want a room each of course. May we see them?'

They did not have to move far because on the left side of the hallway were two of the vacant rooms. In the first there was little room for the mattress that was leaning up against the curtained bay window - an unusual theme. A scratched upright piano, minus piano stool, hugged one of the peeling walls. The room looked as if it had been unoccupied for several months and it was easy to see the dust floating in the air between the door and the ray of light penetrating the gap in the curtains. It was not a good start. The second was sparsely furnished with only a double bed giving it a roomier feeling, though rather peculiarly the bed had two mattresses on its divan base. There was a long, narrow sash window in the corner of the room and an unused open fireplace. Although it looked just as unloved, it was not quite as dusty as the first room.

Judy decided that it wasn't going to get much better. 'I suppose this one is not too bad and if I could move some of that other furniture in here -'

'There are more rooms upstairs,' muttered Russell, mounting the creaking steps several at a time.

Upstairs there was a brighter feel to the house with one modern bedroom at the back end of the corridor, beyond a bright and airy bathroom. The little room was non-descript with white walls and a light brown fitted carpet, yet it had the feel of a room that was used regularly, unlike the two downstairs.

'Oh!' exclaimed Christine. 'I like this room very much. I shall have this room.' As if to confirm her decision, she sat down on the single bed.

'Hang on. Maybe I want it.'

'But Judy you chose the second room. You didn't ask me if I wanted it.'

There was an awkward silence broken at last, by Judy. 'Anymore?' *Her* room no longer seemed better than the one at the front of the house. She was hopeful when the young man nodded.

Back towards the front of the house, there was a cold, bare room situated directly above the second viewed room. Looking at the cracked window, Judy pulled a face and he shut the door again.

'And that's our room,' he stated, with a peculiar note of pride in his monotone voice betraying a slight Scottish accent. 'It stretches across the whole width of the house.'

'Oh well. I'll stay downstairs then.'

'Where does that lead to?' asked Christine, noticing the narrow single panel door opposite the room they had just viewed.

'That goes up to the attic room, but I doubt you'll want it as there is no bed up there,' he said.

'Has anyone ever used it?' asked Judy.

'Oh yeah. It's a cool room. The last person hasn't long moved out,' Russell told them.

'So, what did he, or she, sleep on?' Judy continued.

'Badger was a tough nut,' Russell said. 'He didn't need a bed. He just slept on a rolled-up piece of foam. You really wouldn't like it.'

'I'd like to see it anyway?' she demanded, 'There are plenty of mattresses around to take up there.'

Walking up the steep and narrow staircase leading to the attic room, it was difficult to see how they would get a mattress up there, or indeed, anything that didn't roll up. Once up there, all three had to stand close together to fit in the tiny room with its low sloped ceiling. The only item of furniture was an old wicker chair behind the door. The creaking floorboards were covered with a faded, matted brown carpet that wrinkled at several points. The tiny iron-latched window gave the room a charm that the other rooms lacked. There was definitely something special about the room.

'What's that?' Christine said, pointing to a miniature cupboard door built into the wall beneath the window.

Russell looked at the cupboard and shrugged his shoulders. 'Dunno. I've never noticed it before now.'

Judy knelt down and pulled the tiny wooden door open at which point a chilly, musty-smelling breeze brushed past her.

Christine, though standing a few feet away, shivered. 'Oh, did you feel that? It was as cold as the grave.'

'It'll be a draught coming from a broken roof tile or something similar,' said Russell. 'Anyway, do you still want this room?'

After shaking her head Judy began to follow Russell and Christine back down the short narrow flight of stairs. Then she felt something icy touch her on the shoulder. It seemed more physical than a draft. It felt like a hand, but she knew that there was nothing there, so she didn't turn around even though the feeling remained until she had closed the single panel door behind her.

The following day, the two women moved into the house. Looking at the double bed in her room, Judy wondered why it had two mattresses and she lay down on it to see how it felt. It was surprisingly comfortable. Then she dragged one of the mattresses off and lay down once again to see how the other mattress was. Finding it full of broken springs and protruding wires she dragged the other mattress back to its former place. There's always a reason, she thought to herself, as she threw a cotton sheet over the high mound.

Christine's head appeared around the door, and she feigned a gasp of surprise.

'Ooh, you have been remarkably busy Judy. You have transformed this room.'

'Very funny Christine,' Judy replied. 'Whoever was in this room before me probably made the best use of it, so I'll leave it as it is for now. Time for a cuppa. I've got some chocolate digestives here. How is your room?'

'I love it. It's perfect. I'm so pleased with it,' she answered.

'Alright. It's okay but it's far from perfect.'

'Your room is nice too,' Christine said, with a grin.

Judy grinned back. 'No, it's not. It's bloody awful.'

Russell and his girlfriend Tess were about to go out, but they accepted Christine's offer of tea and a get to know each other chat.

'So how long have you both lived here?' asked Judy, trying to ignore the particularly annoying broken spring beneath her.

'Two years, though Russell has been here longer.'

Tess, like Russell, was about twenty, with luscious long dark hair worn in a side plait, and a perfectly made-up face. She was wearing a black minidress with thigh-length boots. They were an attractive couple, Judy thought, but so much of that was down to youth. Wait till they were closer to thirty.

'So, you met in this house,' remarked Christine, while carefully watching the chocolate biscuit she had dipped in her tea. It was her fourth biscuit. 'How sweet!' Though a few years younger than Judy, Christine felt no connection to the couple's age group either. She had little time for the trendy student image.

'We don't see ourselves as a sweet couple,' Tess laughed. 'You should have seen the state of this house while ten students were living here. It was hardly romantic.'

'Ten! Where did you all sleep?' Judy realized, as soon as she had asked the question, that they were in typical student accommodation. No wonder the young man looked bemused when they viewed the house.

'Most used it as a pied à Terre,' Tess replied. 'There were rarely more than eight people here at any one time.'

'Why did they all move out? Why are we the only four people living here now?' Christine sounded suspicious.

Russell, quiet up till then, suddenly entered the conversation. 'They've all graduated and moved on. We're leaving too at the end of the week.'

'But that means it will be just me and Christine living here, in this huge house,' Judy cried. 'What about bills? We can't afford to keep it going between us?'

'Don't worry,' Russell said. 'The rent is still inclusive of bills. This house has never been full, well at least not for a year. I don't think people like the area. It's too quiet. The landlord doesn't mind as long as it is occupied. If it stays empty too long, it risks squatters moving in, like in the neighbouring houses.'

'Squatters,' Christine cried. 'Where? Not in this house?'

'Of course, not in this house, as long as it is occupied, but sometimes they break into the other houses in the terrace; although they are moved on quickly enough.'

'Doesn't anybody live in the houses next door?' Christine asked, slightly confused.

'The ones further down are rented too, I think. But the others are so run down, the owners could never get permission to let them out. Every now and again a chancer will furnish one and let it out illegally but it's never long before the authorities catch up.'

'You never said you were moving out when you were showing us around,' said Judy. It was as much an accusation as a comment.

'We didn't know then,' Russell protested. 'A mate of ours has a room to spare in his house and it's closer to the university. It will give us an extra twenty-minute sleep.'

There was an awkward silence while the four people sipped on their tea. Then Tess attempted to break the ice when she turned to face Judy.

'Why don't you move into our room when we go? It's big enough to be a bedsit. You must feel a bit like a squatter in that other room.'

'Oh!' Judy frowned. She hadn't. Then she thought of moving into that big, bright bedroom with two large windows and spreading across the whole width of the house. 'Well, there's no point in leaving the best room empty and it'll be good to have some furniture,' she laughed.

Christine said nothing.

After the young couple had gone out, the two women looked at each other.

'Do you think we should try to find some more people to rent the rooms?' Christine suggested. 'I don't think I would have agreed to take it if I had known that we were going to be the only two people living here.'

'I know what you mean, especially if there's a chance of squatters moving into the empty rooms. Can you think of anyone who might be interested? I only really know people at work, and I can't see them wanting to live here. What about one of your many friends?'

'No Judy. None of them would live in a place like this.'

As often happened, the atmosphere turned on a sixpence.

'And yet you live here, Christine.'

'Judy, do you honestly think I want to live here? As soon as I find somewhere better to live, I will be gone. You seem quite happy to live anywhere.'

'No, I'm not. We had to find a place quickly and it was this or the street.'

'But you were only looking for two rooms, Judy. It limited our options.'

'Yes. I was looking. You couldn't be bothered. Why should I look for a house for just you?'

'Don't worry. I'll do my own looking in the future. In fact, I'll start today.'

Despite her bravado, it was a blow to Judy; Christine was thinking of moving on without her. Although the two women were far from being close friends, while their living situation was the same, Judy did not feel so miserable about her own life. In a week she would be thirty years old, single, friendless, with a part-time job and renting a room in a scruffy house. She tried to lighten the mood by offering to make another cup of tea, but Christine was not ready to back down.

'Not for me. I'm going out and I don't think I shall be back tonight. My friends have invited me over to watch a film and I'll probably stay. Enjoy your evening.'

London, 1920

The shrill ringing of the bell could barely be heard once the cries and laughter started, and a bubbling stream of young children rushed out to play in the small, rectangular yard of the orphanage. The high wrought-iron gates were there to keep out unwelcome intruders, yet they added to the building's grim appearance. It did not resemble a place of fun, more a prison. The children running around the concrete area immediately behind the gates were the youngest occupants, while those older than ten were inside, helping with the domestic tasks required in the running of the charitable institution in which they lived and learned.

Upstairs, away from the excitement of the younger children, two girls of about fifteen were arguing over which one should have the unenviable job of sweeping out the fireplace. It was a dirty and dusty chore that caused whoever did it to sneeze and cough for the following few hours, and neither girl was prepared to give in.

Suddenly, one of the girls picked up a sweeping brush and pushed it gently into the other girl's face. 'That decides it. Now you have dust up your nose anyway, you might as well clean the wretched thing.'

Despite her dirty face, the other girl laughed and, picking up a poker, held it up in the air as though preparing for a duel. For the next couple of minutes, the girls played at fencing, the absurdity of the broomstick adding to the sense of hilarity. They could have been actors on a stage. Each girl twirled around and jumped backward then sideways into the dormitory, where they tossed off their shoes and leapt onto the narrow beds.

Was it the dust in one girl's eye that caused what happened next, or did she misread the other girl's movement? It was a moment in time that had a lifelong impact. Suddenly, the whiteness of the bedsheets that the girl with the broomstick stood on began to be dotted with red. The fun had turned to horror when the tip of the

22

poker pierced the girl's abdomen and her opponent watched as the peppering of red was now a single indistinct shape. She dropped the poker and started screaming as her friend collapsed into a small pool of her own blood.

Chapter Three

Faced with spending her first night in the new house alone, Judy tried not to care that she hadn't been invited to the film-watching night. Even though they were Cristine's friends rather than hers, Emma in particular, always made an effort to welcome her into their trendy group. Christine liked to act as the gatekeeper to any social event that included them. She always made Judy feel as if she should be grateful for any invite to be in their precious company.

Looking in the mirror, Judy's eyes settled on the faint lines near her round brown eyes, then past her freckled button nose and down to her bow-shaped mouth, thankful at least that there was no sign of grey in her long, black curly hair. She knew she was still pretty and wondered if the reason Christine could be so mean was that she was jealous. Sure, Christine was stylish like all French women, but she didn't turn heads. Christine was always bragging about men looking at her, but they really weren't.

Just to pass some time she had a second look at the other bedrooms in the house. To her irritation, Christine had already managed to unpack all her things, leaving her room looking neat and feminine in a subtle way, just as she looked. Somehow, Christine didn't have to try too hard to give finesse to the most basic room. Judy pulled open the wardrobe door to find an orderly row of light-coloured tops and trousers hanging on the rail and a collection of similar flat shoes on the floor. How was it that

Christine only had to wrap a silk scarf around her neck and suddenly she was Juliette Binoche? Of course, men looked at her.

Next she moved onto the front bedroom and found that Russell was right. It was a lovely big room that had an air of grandeur about it. For the first time Judy could appreciate how the house had once looked, before the decades of multiple occupancies had tarnished its memory. The young couple had creatively furnished the room with wall hangings, furry rugs, and fairy lights, and there were several bean bags scattered on the huge floor. It was a fabulous room and Judy was looking forward to it being hers.

Back in her own room Judy suddenly felt a bit scared. Walking around upstairs had reminded her how large the house was, and that she was on her own in it. As she was undressing, she glanced at the fireplace, thinking she heard something. Any sound she heard during the night would terrify her. She switched on the radio, setting the volume at just the right level to distract her from any other noises. Schuman's Scenes from Childhood. Perfect.

Judy woke up to an icy chill in the room. She looked at her watch. Three o'clock. There must be a crack in her window too, she thought. Then her heart jumped on hearing something moving in the room. At least it sounded as though it were in the room. Too scared to move she strained her ears to decipher any noise that was not coming from the melodic piano notes on the radio which was still on. There it was again, near the fireplace. So close to her. Shuffling. Scraping. Her heart was pounding. She did not know whether to run for the door or pull the duvet over her head. A few minutes passed until the sounds stopped and there was an eerie silence. Then there was another sound, a different, unmistakable sound - a baby crying. It was muffled and Judy couldn't tell if it was coming from behind the chimney breast or outside of the bedroom window. She lay listening for ten minutes or so until she could listen no more. Although the baby's cries were disturbing, they were not as threatening as the first sounds and, telling herself it was probably

25

an urban fox, she no longer felt that she was in danger. After turning up the volume on the radio, Judy pulled the duvet over her head and waited for sleep to arrive.

When Christine came home there was a young man with her. Saying nothing to Judy, they both climbed the stairs and Judy heard the bedroom door close. She could hear their muffled voices above her as she made herself a drink in the kitchen. He didn't look like one of Emma's group as his six o'clock shadow was too unkept to be designer. She knew Christine was not averse to the occasional one-night stand but was puzzled as to the pickup place. Was he a gate-crasher or someone she'd met at the bus stop? The bedroom door opened again, and she heard footsteps coming back down the stairs.

'I have a new boyfriend,' Christine announced, on entering the kitchen. His name is Gary, and he will be here a few times a week. You don't mind, do you?'

'Of course not. He doesn't have to stay in your room, Christine. I'm happy for you both to use the sitting room,' she lied. 'Where did you meet him?'

'In the Arms. He was with his friends, and they started chatting with us. I arranged to meet him in the café this morning, you know, your favourite café. I think I like him.'

'So you went to the pub. I thought it was a film night.'

'The film was bad, so we decided to go out instead. Why shouldn't we?' Christine responded, with defiance.

Suddenly they became aware of the man standing in the doorway, staring at the two women with a bemused expression on his face.

'Judy, this is Gary. Gary this is Judy. She lives here too.' There was no mention of 'friend'.

The man called Gary did not respond to Christine's introduction. Rather, he acted as though Judy were invisible.

'I'm going now,' he muttered. 'I'll come round tonight.' Then he walked away without another word.

Christine followed him out to the front door. Judy could hear her whispering something to her guest before returning to the kitchen. Accepting there was no point in sulking, Judy decided to change the subject.

'Have you heard any strange noises in this house?'

'What do you mean by strange noises?'

'Last night I could hear shuffling noises coming from the chimney breast, then a baby crying. And my room felt cold, well, not cold exactly, but icy. I can't really explain the feeling.'

'It was probably the wind, or you were imagining it. Those noises might be normal for this area. You just haven't heard them before. I've heard that a fox can make the same sound as a baby crying.'

'Yes that's what I thought yet it felt as though it was coming from inside, rather than outside.'

'If there had been anyone in your bedroom you would have seen them. I'm sure you were just nervous because there was no one else here. Well, you will have to get used to it Judy as there will be other nights when I am not here. Anyway, Gary is coming around later so I must get ready. I don't suppose you will be going out anywhere tonight.'

The laughter emanating from the sitting room might as well have been artillery fire. Judy had eaten her microwave dinner at the kitchen table and was now standing near the door, wishing there was another way through to her bedroom. Then she reprimanded herself. If this was how things were going to be, she had better break the ice sooner rather than later. She pledged to herself that she would make every effort to be friendly. Despite the self-reassurance, she found herself holding her breath before slowly releasing it as she opened the kitchen door.

The new American comedy Friends was just finishing, and the couple's attention switched from the television screen to Judy entering the room. Christine and Gary were both sitting on the same chair, Christine on his lap, her tight-sleeved arms wrapped around his neck. For a split second, an excruciating silence filled the space until Christine spoke.

'Oh! You've made yourself tea. Would you like a tea, Gary?'

The man nodded without looking up.

Christine's cheerful humming could be heard from the kitchen as Judy settled on the edge of the settee. Remembering her pledge just a few seconds earlier, Judy made a psychological step forward by breaking the silence.

'Is it funny? I heard you both laughing.' The words struggled to crawl out of her mouth. Had she even made a sound?

'Eh!' Gary looked taken aback by Judy's conversation starter.

'Friends. Was it very funny? Or were you laughing at something else?' Judy enquired, far too quickly and she immediately regretted the implication of her second question – were they laughing at her?

'Dunno,' he replied. 'Chris finds it funny. I wasn't really watching it.' Silence once again. Judy sighed gently to herself and turned back to face the television screen, wishing the adverts would finish. That was the problem with those glamorous American programmes, she thought. They seemed to bring with them the endless commercials common in the United States.

'So where do you sleep?' Gary's question almost made Judy jump. Now it was her turn to be taken aback.

'In the room next door, the second one from the front door. It's not that comfortable so I don't spend too much time in there, except to sleep of course'

'Is that all?' he asked, with an unnerving stare.

Was he flirting? She hadn't really looked at him before as he was usually entwined with Christine. He was attractive in a roguish way. Not her type, but it gave her a smug feeling that Christine's new boyfriend had wandering eyes. In fact, maybe she had been a bit too quick to call him her boyfriend.

'I'm sorry. I should have offered you a drink, but we don't usually bother asking each other. Only after we've had enough of arguing. You must think me rude.'

'Nah., I didn't even notice your tea,' he replied, still staring. Another suggestive comment? Finding herself blushing, she turned back to the adverts.

'Shall we…?' Christine had returned from the kitchen and was gesturing Gary towards the hall. He got up and followed her into the hall and up the stairs.

Had Judy noticed an accusatory glare from her before she left the room? Although she had hardly been flirting, Judy bet herself that she wouldn't be left alone with Gary again, as she heard Christine giggling before the bedroom door closed.

Back in her own company Judy relaxed into the large settee, feeling the already familiar broken springs coming up to meet her. Gary's leather jacket lay crumpled in a heap on the arm of the settee next to where she was sitting. It had been raining heavily all day, so she felt it to see if it was still wet, which it was. She picked it up intending to move it to the now vacant chair, however, as she held it awkwardly, something dropped out of one of the pockets. Bouncing on the carpet, the object then slid, as these things always do, under the settee.

Horrified, Judy threw down her half-empty cup and sank to the floor to look for it. If they came back into the room, she would have to explain why she was moving it. Would they believe her? Christine would be sure to make her feel stupid somehow. Judy placed her cheek flat against the filthy carpet and peered into the inch and a half gap underneath the settee. There it was, about six inches back from the edge. Stretching her hand under the wooden frame she just managed to grasp the cold steely object and pulled it out. She gasped. Was it a pen knife? She hadn't seen one for a few years. On further examination it was clear that it was not a penknife as there was no corkscrew, nail file, or any other miniature tool. It was a flick knife. She dropped it once again but this time it fell into the middle of the room. Judy had never seen a weapon before, apart from in museums and once when she was on holiday in Spain, and that was on a policeman.

Suddenly Christine's boyfriend took on a sinister appearance and his suggestive comments gave Judy the creeps. Picking up the knife, she fumbled with the jacket, trying to locate the pocket from which it came, but there were several, inside and out. Which pocket had the knife been in? She took a guess and slotted it into one of the inside pockets, feeling as she did another object. Looking at it more closely, she saw it was a credit card – American Express. She didn't have to look at the name. Gary was an unskilled factory worker. This wasn't his card.

Glasgow, May 1939

Eveline wrapped the hunk of bread and margarine in paper, took an apple from the fruit bowl, and handed them to her husband who was already halfway down the communal stairs.

'Don't forget your dinner, dear,' she said softly, kissing him lightly on the lips. Her dark hair hung limply around her unwashed neck, and she pulled the strands away as he stood back to look at her properly.

'Thanks, love, but I don't think these will last till then. I'm famished,' he said, smiling.

'I'm sorry there was no breakfast. It'll be different tomorrow. I promise,' she called, as he disappeared out of sight.

Closing the door after him, she then sat down in front of the fire and poured herself a cup of warm tea from the china teapot covered with the woollen cosy she had knitted herself. The tea cosy had started to unravel from the bottom, yet another thing she had failed to complete. She had been up since dawn and had already scrubbed clean the blood-stained sheets which were hanging next to her in front of the fire. The meagre heat emitting from the coals was tempered further by the dampness of the laundry and the windowpane was disappearing under a blanket of steam.

Yesterday had been a difficult day. Eveline had spent most of it in bed, recovering from her sixth miscarriage. She had never passed the first trimester and remained childless. It was a lesson never learned. There was only her and her younger sister left after their parents had both died of the Spanish Flu, leaving the girls to be brought up in an orphanage. A family not blessed with good fortune should not seek to pass their burden down through more generations.

She often wished that she too had been part of the cruel cull of the 1919 disease, a victim of nature, her life out of her hands. Whereas now she was at the mercy of her own decisions, as well as fate. James desperately wanted children and Eveline felt guilty every time she experienced the familiar stabbing pains in her stomach. However, after the physical and mental agony of the following hours, there was always a part of her that felt relief. Relief that she would not have another person's future in her hands. Relief that she would not die and leave a child without its mother. Relief that someday, somehow, she could leave this grim tenement and never return.

Chapter Four

As Judy approached the house, she found herself glancing up at the attic window where she noticed something dark within the small, rectangular pane. She could have sworn it was the silhouette of a woman's head. Perhaps a new tenant was looking around, she thought. Yet there was no sign of Russell's car and Tess was away for a few days, so who would be showing them around? The other possibility was that Christine must have also come home for lunch, though it was not clear how she could get home without Judy. She reminded herself that Christine didn't go anywhere unless she was chauffeur driven. Looking across at the heavily draped bay window she made a mental note to give the room a spring clean when she had time. It might brighten up the atmosphere of the entrance hall which was hardly welcoming.

'Christine. Are you back?'

There was no reply. Christine always left her housekey and handbag in the same spot on the kitchen worktop, something that irritated Judy, but there was no sign of either item. Strange, she thought. So, who had she seen in the upstairs window a few minutes ago? After making a sandwich, she went upstairs.

The attic room was still and silent when she opened the door. In the starkness of daylight, it was clearly empty and undisturbed, yet something was wrong, something was different. Her eyes studied each part of the room separately: the old wicker chair in one corner, the small wooden window, the bare ragged carpet that covered the floor of the room. Then she saw that the little hatch door of the cupboard under the window was slightly open. Had it been open when she came in? Of course, it must have been.

She walked across the room towards the tiny door to shut it properly but, as she grabbed the little handle, a slight movement inside made her jump. Opening the door wider, she saw something small and square on the floor inside. Tentatively, she reached into the dark space, picked up the flat object, and examined it. It was a black and white photograph of a middle-aged woman standing upright in front of a sideboard. The woman was wearing a dark dress, her dark hair was tied back in a harsh bun, and her expression was stern. Or maybe it was sad. She turned the photograph around to see the words 'Eveline, Glasgow 1941' written on the back. Judy thought for a second. Her shadow could have caused an obscuring of the light which then gave the impression of movement, she told herself. Yet she was certain that the space had been empty when they first viewed the room. She replaced the photograph and closed the little door quickly, suddenly wishing she had not been quite so brave as to enter the attic room while alone in the house. Counting to ten, she made a brisk retreat out of the room and down the stairs, closing the single panel door behind her. She picked up her sandwich and left the house.

Christine found it difficult to concentrate during her morning lessons as she couldn't stop thinking about Gary. Judy was going to drop her off at his house on the way home from work and she found herself nervous and excited at the same time. She knew he was a bit rough but there was something about his broodiness that she found irresistible. If the relationship was going to develop, they would have to spend most of the time at her house. He had told her he lived in an overcrowded house, sharing his bedroom with another man. Staying there was out of the question.

What would Gary make of Judy who never went out or had any friends of her own to visit? And would they have to spend most of the time in Christine's bedroom which was hardly suitable with its single bed? It was a shame that Judy would be moving into the front bedroom as it was large enough to have a living space as well as a bed. They could use some of the spare furniture in the unused rooms to make it more of a bedsit. Perhaps Judy would agree to move into Christine's small room. After all, it was the nicest room, even though it was small.

Later that day she was sitting next to Judy while the battered Fiesta manoeuvred its way through the crazy rush hour traffic.

'You like my room, don't you Judy?'

The leading question did not have the desired effect as Judy knew exactly what Christine was angling for.

'It's a bit small but it is okay. Why do you ask?'

'I thought the large front room would be perfect for Gary and me to use as a sitting-room and bedroom. It would free up the downstairs sitting room for you.'

'Oh, I don't think so Christine. I've been picturing myself in that bedroom since Tess mentioned it. I love the fact that it is the entire width of the house. You could always move into my room when I vacate it.'

Christine did not respond but switched on the radio and turned the dial until the violins were replaced by a man speaking:

Police are appealing for witnesses after a young woman was attacked near Hackney underground station last night. The victim was taken to the local hospital where her condition is said to be stable.

Judy switched it off. 'I hate the news.'

'But that's near us. We need to know what's happening?'

'They are always trying to scare us. Probably think we should still be tied to the kitchen sink with husbands to protect us.'

Christine sighed. Would Judy be so brave without her car?

They pulled up outside what could best be described as a common lodging house. A group of men were standing in the front garden, each holding a can of beer in one hand and a cigarette in the other. They all turned their attention to the women in the car.

'Enjoy your evening, Christine.'

Russell and Tess were gone when Judy got back to the house at five o'clock. She felt a warm glow of optimism building in her chest as she pictured herself occupying the best room of the house to the envy of Christine. She'd regret jumping in and grabbing that back room so early as she couldn't now insist on a second bite of the cherry. How dare she think she is entitled to it just because she has a boyfriend? Let's get up there quickly, she thought, planning on making the room her own by the time Christine got home. She would give it a good clean then tomorrow she would go shopping and buy herself a new duvet cover and some pot pourri to give it a feminine ambience – and remove the smell of cannabis. There would be no more jokes about her room being like a squat. Even Christine's friends would jump at the chance to have it.

She opened the bedroom door filled with excitement, still planning how she would personalise every square inch of it. But she stopped in the doorway. Now it was unoccupied, the room appeared larger than before, the two large windows filtering much light into the vast rectangular space which now seemed much too big. There were two hefty wooden wardrobes at opposite ends of the room, one to the left of the door and the other to the right. A large double bed sat unmade, exposing its old and battered mattress. The bed was situated immediately behind the door and rested on a faded mustard-patterned carpet that stretched from wall to wall. Now the soft furnishings were gone, it bore little resemblance to the warm and trendy room that she had peeped into just the other day.

Judy glanced back at each wardrobe and an uneasy sensation crept through her body. Why did it feel as though they were watching her – like two sentries guarding the room? Oh, for heaven's sake, she thought, they were inanimate objects. She stepped forward intending to open each door fully, but a nagging feeling stopped her. The room suddenly felt so unwelcoming she knew she could not move into it; it didn't want her inside. The hairs prickled on the back of her neck; her optimism gone. No windows were open, but the room was devoid of any warmth. It was as though no one had been inside it for years, let alone a couple of hours earlier.

As she closed the bedroom door, she wondered how it had seemed so much more pleasant when the young couple used it. Why had it accepted their presence but not hers? She scalded herself for imagining that the room had its own mind. Oh well, she thought, at least being downstairs she was near the front door. She smiled as she pictured Christine alone upstairs, and she would make sure she told her about her experience in the big bedroom. Gary wouldn't be with her every night, or he would have to pay rent. Christine would be alone upstairs in that creepy empty room and Judy comforted herself with that thought, small though it was.

If Christine had hoped that the men were outside because it was a non-smoking house, she was to be bitterly disappointed. Inside was the unmistakable smell of cannabis which made her heave.

'Perhaps we should go out somewhere,' she suggested to Gary, as they climbed the second staircase to his attic room.

'It's late and I'm whacked. Don't worry. My roommate is dossing in another room tonight. We've got an arrangement.'

'How romantic!'

'Lighten up, Chrissie. Come here.' Gary pulled Christine into his arms and began kissing her.

'Okay, but let us at least get into your stinking bedroom,' she replied, with a grin.

An hour later, Gary having disappeared downstairs, Christine was having a closer look around the room. A cheap acoustic guitar hung on a hook above the bed, and she instinctively plucked a few strings to calm her nerves. Then she walked over to the boxes in the corner, filled with clothes, books, and cassette tapes. She pulled out the tapes in the hope of finding something to play. Jimi Hendrix, Eric Clapton, Pink Floyd. That would be a no, she decided. Underneath she noticed a black woollen object and she smiled to herself. He had been wearing that hat when she first met him, and she thought he looked like Johnny Depp. She pulled it out of the box and held it to her nose but at that point, she realized it was too long to be the hat. Looking more closely, she saw three large holes in it. What on earth, she thought, dropping it onto the floor.

Just then the door opened, and Gary walked in carrying two cereal bowls and two mugs on a tray.

'Hey. Found anything you like? There's no George Michael I'm afraid.'

Christine looked confused for a moment then remembered the cassette tapes.

'Gary, why do you have a balaclava?'

'A what? Oh, that's not mine. Karl must have hidden it in my box. No idea what he uses it for though. Come on. Dinner is served.'

It seemed like a plausible explanation, so Christine sat back on the bed and accepted the bowl of pasta mixed with what appeared to be tomato soup. At least there was grated cheese on it.

London, May 1939

It had been her husband's idea. Something to keep her occupied during the day while he was at work. A little project for her.

'It can't be too difficult to find her, darling' he had said, over breakfast one morning. 'You know she went to Haworth to work so start by sending a letter there to enquire as to her current whereabouts. She may still be there.' He picked up his medical bag, kissed her on the cheek then left her alone for the rest of the day.

Bertha picked up her wedding photograph which took pride of place on their solid oak sideboard. They were a handsome couple, both tall and slim with dark hair and dark eyes. She hadn't seen her sister for twenty years and had no idea what she looked like now. Even the battered photographs from their childhood had been lost over time. They had looked alike as children but that was a very long time ago.

Would Eveline want to get back in touch with her younger sister after all these years? Would she even be able to read any letter that she received from Bertha? She remembered that Eveline had left school early, but you never unlearn something like reading and writing, she thought. And her elder sister had had such high hopes for her future once she had left their makeshift home. What had become of her life? Had she married one of the rich sons at Haworth? Probably not.

Bertha picked up the dirty crockery from the kitchen table and carried it over to the sink. Her days were interminably dull. Cooking and cleaning. Cooking and cleaning. It was only because she refused to have a maid that she had housework to fill her day. She wished Edward had allowed her to keep working at the hospital, if only part-time. But he wanted his wife to be at home with the family, if it ever comes, she thought. He had even bought her a piano ignoring the fact that she had not played since living at the orphanage. Although a mere child, her piano playing was better than Mrs. Ellis who gave them music lessons and played during assemblies. But she had lost interest as teenagers often do.

'I've forgotten how to play,' she told him dismissively.

'You cannot forget how to play the piano. Have lessons,' he said, as if she were a child.

But piano playing was yet another solitary activity she could do without. Therefore, Bertha decided to visit the local library to look for the address of Haworth.

Chapter Five

'There's something bad at the front of the house. The back is peaceful, fine. But the front, it's ... it's as though every room doesn't want you to be in it. And yet it's the same house. I think the back of the house must be newer. Yes, that's it. It must be an extension. There's no back part to the attic floor.'

'Uh, that's because it's an attic and attics tend to be in the roof.'

'Ok, smart Alec,' quipped Judy, to the woman sitting across the table to her. 'Maybe just the bathroom and kitchen are extended. Oh, and the back bedroom of course.'

She'd bumped into Becky at the petrol station. They'd been on the same residential language course several years earlier but had failed to keep in touch. Although both women had been in a similar situation when they first met, Becky was now settled in a permanent nursing job at an inner-city care home and had even managed to get a foot on the property ladder. The stark contrast in fortune was reflected in their cars - Judy with her old blue Ford Fiesta and Becky, a brand-new Renault Clio. But Judy was pleased to see her and looked forward to catching up. They both drove to the nearest McDonald's to chat over a beaker of coffee. It was refreshing and heartening to speak to someone other than Christine, and Judy promised herself she would make a real effort to stay in touch.

'I'm going outside when I get back to see how they're separated from the front part of the house,' Judy said, while squirting tomato sauce on her breakfast roll.

Becky raised her eyebrows. 'Haven't you noticed already? I mean, when you are outside, haven't you noticed?'

'I haven't been out the back yet believe it or not. There's been no need and anyway, the back door keeps jamming. It's a UPVC door so it must be fairly new.'

'And now for this Madame that you live with. She must start coughing up petrol money or else get the bus like other people who haven't got a car. I can't believe you pick her up and take her to work even when you are not working yourself,' Becky remarked, in a lecturing tone.

'I know. I'm a pushover, but it gets me out of the house. And anyway, there are very few buses the hours she works, and the bus stop is isolated. I suppose I just can't be that cruel. Maybe she'll surprise me and buy me a big birthday present, or a card even.'

'If she doesn't even do that, Judy, you really should stop thinking of her as a friend. She is using you. And it wouldn't be cruelty; it would be self-respect.'

Becky promised to visit Judy when work quietened down a bit and suggested they meet more regularly in the New Year.

'Promise you won't disappear for another year,' she joked.

Judy picked up her car keys and said her goodbyes to her friend. It didn't help when the well-rounded Becky reminded her how she was being taken advantage of by Christine. In the McDonalds carpark the clouds were swirling and there was a chilly breeze in the air. Becky unlocked her car from the shelter of the doorway, said her goodbyes, jumped in her Clio, and tooted the horn as she drove away. The spitting raindrops stung Judy's face as she struggled to insert the car door key at just the right angle for it to open. She now felt more miserable than when she first got to the café. How could that even be?

Christine hadn't slept all night. Gary had agreed to push the other bed against the door which had no lock and it had been enough while they were both awake. But now Gary was fast asleep, and she was thinking about his roommate's balaclava. What was his name? Karl. He said he didn't know anything about his roommate, nor did he care. But she cared right now as she was in Karl's room, and he was somewhere in the house. Why would anyone need a balaclava? London wasn't the South Pole. She'd asked Gary if Karl was Irish, but he had just laughed and told her not to be so prejudiced. But that wasn't the kind of terror that scared her most. Hadn't the police reports said that the victims of their attacker had been unable to see his face?

After several hours Christine was satisfied that no one was going to push their way into the bedroom, yet she still couldn't relax. She wanted to use the toilet but there was no way she was stepping outside the door on her own. It was too early in the relationship for her to share that kind of intimacy with Gary. In any case she had encountered the bathroom earlier and had little desire to return any time soon. The more she thought about the house, the more she wanted to leave. It was time for Gary to wake up and see her safely home. From now on they would stay in her room.

After a struggle the key finally turned to the right and Judy stepped through the back door. The back wall was more than six feet high with an overhang which made it appear even more insurmountable. The pebble-dashed surface was shiny and smooth and painted black, an odd colour few would choose for their garden backdrop. A curious fact was that there was no doorway leading out of the yard which was easily large enough for a vehicle. A parking space in London was as sought after as vacant rooms, and it couldn't even be called a garden as it was. It was more like the outside space of a prison for inmates to breath in the dark damp air that lay below the high walls.

In the bottom left-hand corner stood a concrete shed the height of the wall, its door padlocked with a heavy rusty metal fastening. Near the top a small window with metal bars added to the impenetrable appearance of the shed. She wondered when anyone had last been inside and what if anything lay within the grim walls. Distracted from her initial reason for entering the outside space, Judy looked around for something high enough to stand on in order to look through the concrete shed window.

An old wooden crate lay near the shed door. It was empty so might not hold her weight, but her curiosity persuaded her to push it over to the barred window. She stood tiptoed with just enough balance to peer through the bottom end of the windowpane. The shrivelled up remains of flies peppered the cobweb that curtained the pane. There was no light penetrating the small window, yet something glinted in the darkness that faced her. The mudguard of a bicycle wheel perhaps. There was nothing else visible to her squinting eye save for what appeared to be a crumpled sack that the old bicycle rested upon. A smell of mildew came from the rotting wooden frame, and she wondered how much time had passed since anyone had been inside. By the look of the padlock, no one had opened it for years. Whose bike had been abandoned, she wondered.

Suddenly, a chill ran down the back of Judy's neck. It felt as though she was being watched. She spun around too quickly and stumbled off the crate. Looking back up at the house she saw it for the first time; a two-storey extension stretching out into the yard. Its light pebble-dashed walls marked a modern contrast against the dank, dark stone of the original building, a few feet of which had been left to the side of the extension. Judy was surprised to see a window upstairs in the older part of the house. It was not a standard-sized bedroom window but more like one sometimes found midway on a stairwell, an aesthetic feature rather than one of any practical use. It was peculiar as she couldn't place the window inside the house. Surely it couldn't be boarded up. Why would anyone do that? Perhaps it was rotten like the shed window and the owner didn't want the trouble of replacing it. She tried to picture the precise spot that the window would be from within the house, halfway up the stairs leading to the attic room. Just then her eyes focussed on a raven on the small window ledge as though guarding its property. Was it the raven's eyes that had been watching her just now? She shivered and decided her survey of the backyard was over.

'Don't you even want a drink of something? Tea? Coffee? Water?'

'No, Gary. I've already told you. Just walk me home.'

Christine was looking around the kitchen in horror. The dirty cups, plates, and saucepans piled high in a sink filled with greasy water almost made her cry. Gary had wanted her to help him cook the pasta dish they had eaten the night before, but she had refused, knowing a dirty kitchen would have put her off eating. Last night she didn't want to hurt his feelings. This morning, however, she didn't care.

'Why are you bringing your guitar? You can't carry that the whole distance.'

'I'm meeting a mate in the city and we're doing a bit of busking. Karl's giving me a lift, but he'll drop you off first.'

'What?'

A man in his early forties appeared in the doorway and nodded to Gary, who took Christine by the hand and led her outside. The older man was getting into a battered Escort and before she had a chance to protest, Gary had guided her into the back seat and the car was moving. The car smelt of stale smoke which added to Christine's discomfort. All she wanted to do was get home and have a hot shower, but she could hang on a bit longer.

'Just drop me at the bus stop,' she said, leaning forward slightly. There was no response from either man. It was as though they had forgotten she was in the car.

As they got closer to the house, Christine grew more nervous. She looked at the rear-view mirror and was relieved to see Karl's occasional glances back were directed out of the rear window, and not at her. Was she being paranoid? He hadn't even acknowledged her the whole time she had been in his company. She relaxed for the remainder of the journey.

London, May 1939

So, Bertha wrote a letter to the housekeeper at Haworth and within a week had a reply. The letter informed her that her sister had married James Preece and the couple had moved to Glasgow where he now worked in construction. Fortunately, the housekeeper had included their forwarding address in her letter.

Bertha was surprised at how easy it had been and wondered why she had left it so long. She had been a child when she last saw her sister and now, she was almost middle-aged. It seemed wrong that they had been separated for over half their lives. Suddenly she felt a pang of regret, yet it should not have been up to her. Eveline was the elder sister and had promised to come back, but she had failed to keep her word.

'What a clever wife I have?' her husband, Edward said, when she told him of her successful search.

He suggested that they both take a short holiday to Scotland and make a surprise visit but this idea terrified Bertha. Edward was a truly kind man, and she had no doubt that he loved her regardless of their different upbringing, but she had her pride. For all she knew Eveline and her husband could be living in abject poverty. Just in case, she wanted to assess things before he was introduced, if ever that time should come. Therefore, she wrote another letter, this time directly to her sister.

Chapter Six

There was a familiar drizzle in the night air as Judy and Christine ran towards Judy's car in the college car park. Both women held their breath as Judy turned the ignition key, knowing that the car's engine did not take well to being left in the rain for most of the day. Lurking in the footwell was a can of WD40, ready to be used as a pungent kiss of life on the car's rusty engine. Judy slowly pushed in the choke as they heard the welcome whirring sound of the engine running then, after putting on her glasses, she pulled off. They both relaxed.

'Why haven't you moved into the other bedroom, Judy?' Christine asked. 'Surely, it will be more comfortable than your bedroom, and you were so excited about having a room that stretched the width of the house.'

Judy rubbed a clear circle on the windscreen as they turned onto the high road. 'How can there be both a draft and condensation in this car?'

"Well?" Christine continued to enquire into the reason behind Judy's change of plan. After all, Judy had seemed determined that Christine wouldn't have it.

Judy hesitated before recounting her experience of the previous day and how the room didn't seem to want her in there.

'I know you will say it's just my imagination Christine, and maybe it is, but I'm not moving into that room. I don't care how wide it is,' she said, in an acknowledgement of her own silly boasting. 'You and Gary are welcome to it. That's if you still want it.'

'I don't think I can be bothered now. Although it is funny you should say that about it being spooky. When I was in the kitchen yesterday, the kettle just started to boil on its own even though I was nowhere near it. Do you think kettles can do that? It was really scary because I was in the house by myself.'

There was a moment of silence as though both were deep in thought.

'Maybe that's it,' Judy said finally. 'It's only when we are on our own that we can sense things, though the kettle coming on itself is more than a sensation, I suppose. We could ask the electricity company if it's possible for electrical items to switch themselves on.'

The way Judy had phrased her last remark made the kettle incident appear even more worrying and for a few minutes, the two women shared their misgivings about their new home. They discussed the chill of the attic as well as the unlived-in atmosphere of the rest of the house though Judy's experiences were more numerous than Christine's.

'I wonder whether it's because the house is so empty,' Judy suggested. 'Perhaps it'll be better when other people move in, that's if anyone else does move in. Anyway, I'm sure we'll get used to it. On a happier note, there's a new Indian restaurant that's just opened in town,' she said cheerfully, 'so I thought that we could go there for my birthday next week. What do you think, Chris?'

'I don't like curry. It gives me a bad stomach and the smell stays on my clothes for days. Can't we just have a drink in the house?'

'Oh come on, Christine. It is a special birthday, so I'd rather go out somewhere even if it is just to the pub. What about a pizza?'

'What is the point of spending money sitting in a restaurant when we can sit at home eating the same thing, I'll think about going to the pub for your birthday, but I have a boyfriend now, so I'll be spending much of my time with him.'

'As if I hadn't noticed that you have a boyfriend. He's around the house all the time but I don't complain. I'm not asking much Christine, and I would do the same for you.'

'But I would not ask you to do the same thing for me, Judy. That is the difference between us. And I'm sorry if you think Gary being around is something to complain about. It's entirely normal for me to have my boyfriend stay. You really need to get your own social life instead of relying on me to take you places. I'm not responsible for you. Why would you want to celebrate being thirty anyway?'

The two women avoided each other for the rest of the evening. Christine spent a couple of hours trying on different combinations of her sweaters and trousers with the new scarves she had bought earlier in the day. Meanwhile Judy tried to care about the trials and tribulations of Julia Roberts and Denzel Washington in the Friday night blockbuster movie on television.

She wondered if a life fraught with danger would be worth living if it were spent in the company of a strong, handsome man who saw it as his duty to save you from all evil. How different things would be if there was someone to share the good and bad times with. But life wasn't like the movies, and, if she were the heroine in a thriller, she would probably be left protecting herself. No matter, she told herself, if she had learnt anything in her thirty years, it was that the best place to find a helping hand was at the bottom of one's arm. That was how she had got through most of her life, and she didn't expect things to change.

She heard Christine coming down the stairs and making a phone call, presumably to Gary but then slamming the receiver down without speaking. So much for *I have a boyfriend now*, Judy said to herself, quite aware that her voice would probably carry into the hallway. Maybe he wasn't quite ready to be that boyfriend yet. It said a lot that Christine no longer wanted the front room for a love nest.

When Christine entered the sitting room she looked at the television screen, and, seeing the glamourous actors in the film, sat down to watch it. She loved American shows but that wasn't her main objective. It wasn't often that she felt guilty, but she knew she had been spiteful earlier when refusing to celebrate Judy's birthday.

Maybe Gary wasn't as keen on her as she had hoped. He clearly preferred to go out with his mates than spend the evening with her. Somehow, she didn't believe his story about his friend needing a shoulder to cry on. And he hadn't seemed all that enthusiastic when she had mentioned moving into the large bedroom. It was probably wise for her to be less clingy. Perhaps she would go out for a meal with Judy, or at least buy her a present. However, before having a chance to make amends, she heard something outside the back of the house.

'Did you hear that?'

No answer.

'Judy. Did you hear that sound coming from outside? It sounded like a woman screaming.'

'I'm trying to concentrate. Why don't you ask your boyfriend to investigate?'

'Now you are being childish. I can't help it if you don't have one.'

'I'd rather wait until somebody decent comes along, thank you.'

'You will be waiting forever then. No one decent would have the patience to put up with you and your ways.'

'At least I have standards.'

'You call them standards. That is a joke. You need to take a good look at yourself, Judy. Every time I go out with my friends you come too, and you spoil everything. I take you with me because I feel sorry for you with your pathetic life, but you never try to be friendly. I feel like I am taking along a simpleton who does not know how to speak properly. My friends think you are weird, and they laugh about you, but it is not funny to me. Well, that is the last time you come out with me. You stay with yourself like the strange, unfriendly woman you are. You should always be alone so that you cannot spoil other people's enjoyment.'

Judy fought back the tears of anger pushing through the ducts in her eyes. Did she really deserve that torrent of abuse? Christine could be cruel, but she had crossed a boundary and could never take back those harsh words. Turning back to the film, the plot long escaped from her grasp, she knew there was only one way she could strike back.

An unsettled Christine looked out of her bedroom window, seeing nothing but the vague contours where concrete lines met the natural sky. Had it been a scream or just her imagination? It was silent now. Not even a streak of moonlight broke through the darkness. She wouldn't want to be walking around at night in this area. At night-time, it was hard to believe she was living in London, the epicentre of the world. Where were the bright lights and all-night revellers? The theatres, restaurants, and nightclubs? The nearest bar, the Arms, was a pub that wouldn't look out of place in any mining village in the 1980s. Her sister had been so envious of her moving to 'the big smoke' and was desperate to visit her. Not while she was living in this dump though.

The moon made a brief appearance through the curtain of dark clouds, throwing a shaft of light down into the yard. A pair of eyes stared back at her. She jumped, throwing the curtains back across the window. Her heart banging against her chest, she switched off the dim bedroom light and moved back to the window. If someone was outside, they would have to call the police. Although she didn't look forward to speaking to Judy after calling her strange, it would give them a chance to bury the hatchet. What if it was Karl? He now knew where she lived, and Gary might have told him there were just two women in the house.

Pulling the curtains apart, she peered through the gap, standing back slightly as though half expecting a face to be directly behind the window. The moon was withdrawing back behind its cover but there was enough light to notice something else. Something seemed to be glinting through the shed window. It must be something inside, she thought. That was what she thought had been eyes, surely. She closed the curtains and went to bed.

Glasgow, May 1939

When Eveline received the morning post she was intrigued to see what looked very much like a personal, handwritten letter amongst the usual brown envelopes. She examined the handwriting which was elegant and written with care and was addressed to her personally, not Mr. and Mrs. Preece. It was the first letter that she had received as an individual since she had been married. She opened the envelope and took out the letter inside.

Dear Eveline,

I am sure this letter will be a surprise to you, but I hope it won't be unwelcome. I took the liberty of getting your address from your former place of work whereby I also learnt of your marriage. The last memory I have is of you walking away with your little suitcase, a mere girl of fifteen, and that is how I still see you. Although it is an indication of how long we have been parted, I am pleased that you have married and wonder if there are any children, who would, of course, be nephews or nieces of mine.

You might be wondering about my life since I too left St Mary's. I was offered a scholarship to a college to study advanced education. I was a nurse in the local hospital for a few years, until I met my husband, Edward. In fact, it was Edward who persuaded me to contact you as I was unsure that you would want to hear from me after so many years. We have been married ten years but have not as yet been blessed with children. However, we have a lovely little house with a few bedrooms if you and your family ever come down to London.

It is a great regret to me that we were separated at such a young age, particularly at a time when we had only each other, but I have never stopped thinking about you. It would be wonderful to meet sometime in the future if that is agreeable to you and your husband.

I hope you will write to me soon.

With love,

Bertha

Eveline's hands began to shake as the realization hit her – her little sister, whom she had not seen for twenty years, had tracked her down. It had never crossed her mind that she would see Bertha again. The time passing since her departure had dwarfed the years that they had been together. It was as if that time belonged to a different Eveline, an Eveline who she no longer was. Her childhood was a memory that she felt no more part of than the memory of a movie she had watched and not liked very much. She tucked the letter into her apron pocket unsure for that moment how she would respond.

Chapter Seven

When Judy arrived at college, both on time and alone, and shortly before her first class, a couple of her colleagues asked her if everything was okay. They were used to seeing her sitting about for hours on end, waiting for Christine. Sometimes one would remark, in front of Christine, that Judy was too kind for her own good, but the French woman either did not listen or did not care. Well finally the worm had turned, and Judy would start putting her own needs first. She smiled at the thought of Christine queuing at the bus stop in the cold and the rain.

'Let her discover that you cannot get from one place to another with magic beans,' Faye remarked. The matronly teacher cycled a round trip of twenty miles to work every day, rain or shine. 'She's just using you.'

'Some people are leeches,' the other colleague commented.

Judy was shocked at how the others viewed her relationship with Christine. Was it so one-sided? It made her angry and sad at the same time. She thought that for all their disagreements, Christine valued her friendship, at least a little. And Judy would miss her company, particularly as she didn't know anyone else to share a house with. And there were the reports of attacks on women in the area which, up until now, she'd ignored. The college wasn't well lit at night, and it was a lonely walk to the bus stop. Any woman on her own would be likely prey of the dangerous predator. But the acidic comments of the previous night's argument resurfaced, and

Judy's mood turned to just anger. *You spoil everything. You should always be alone.* Okay, she thought, I'll stay away from you.

It was seven-thirty in the evening and the small college was nearing the end of another long day. Christine poured herself a coffee in the cupboard that masqueraded as a staff room at the language school. She gauged every one of her colleagues that were in the room and settled on Reuben, a twenty-something new employee who was a little strange, but then again who wasn't in the world of English language teaching.

He was attractive in a way. Academically scruffy, with his relative youth lending him a trendiness that his more mature peers would not get away with. He wore a light brown Hacking jacket over a pair of scruffy blue corduroy jeans and a white shirt. His curly auburn hair and light beard gave him a Manhattan Jewish look which was extremely popular at that time. Being the only man amongst a group of mostly middle-aged women he couldn't help but stand out in the small crowd. None of that mattered to Christine. What had caught her eye was a set of keys in his hand that included one for a car of some sort.

As the other women began to make their way to their classrooms, she noticed he was slow to move, so she sat down on the chair next to him immediately after it had been vacated.

'Hello,' she said softly. 'May I ask you something? Reuben, isn't it?'

'Yes,' he replied, with what was a slight look of confusion and panic.

'Do you have another class now or are you staying behind to do some preparation?' she asked, giving him no more of an idea as to why she was suddenly speaking to him.

He didn't have another class and he wasn't going to do preparation, but he liked being there in the company of the other staff. He wasn't prepared to admit that though.

'No, I've finished for the day, but I need to photocopy a few things for tomorrow,' he said, preparing himself for what was coming next.

'Could you possibly give me a lift to my bus stop Reuben?' she asked, while looking at him closely so that he could not think too much about what she had said.

'Er, yes, of course. Which bus stop would that be?'

'It's the one on the way out of town, just after the library. It shouldn't take you more than a few minutes. There is a bus leaving at about 9.15 and I will struggle to get there by the time I finish here. If I miss it, I will have to wait an hour for the next bus. I usually come in by car, but my housemate had to be somewhere else. I don't like catching the bus in the dark, but I have no choice tonight.'

Now she was angling for a lift home, he thought. What if she asked straight out? Now he had time to think, he decided he would refuse such a request for the reason being that he had a date. That was a lie but how would she know as she had never shown the slightest interest in him before? For all she knew, he could be engaged or even living with someone.

'I'll wait for you by the entrance,' Christine said, with a smile.

He was cute when he squirmed, and she wondered if he found her attractive too. She could tell from his reaction that he was not greatly confident with women, so he probably did not have a girlfriend. Not that she was interested but it didn't do any harm to wonder.

Reuben's car matched his work persona – scruffy in a trendy way. It was an old Morris 1000 which was cold and uncomfortable inside. On the back seat lay a flask, a sandwich box, and a few library books that were poking out of a hessian bag. Like his car, Reuben's life did not involve much in the way of luxury.

As promised, the journey only took Reuben a few minutes and when they reached the bus stop there were still another ten minutes until the bus was due. There was no one else waiting at the stop. Across the road was a small group of youths who had been huddled around a bench but were now just starting to walk away. Christine couldn't decide whether she would feel safer if they stayed or left. She waited for Reuben to comment but he didn't say anything, and once again she put him on the spot.

'It is very dark and lonely at this bus stop,' she said. 'I don't think it is very safe. I thought there would be more people waiting. Would you mind waiting with me until my bus comes?'

Reuben sighed silently. 'Where do you live? If it is not too much out of the way, I might as well drop you home.'

'That is so kind of you Reuben. I live just before Stepney Green. It is not too far if you go through the back roads. There isn't much traffic this time of night. Of course, I will give you my bus fare.'

'Oh, don't worry,' he replied. 'It is not much out of my way, just a couple of miles.'

Slightly relieved that the next ten minutes or so were settled, it was his turn to be direct.

'So, do you live with Judy? I have seen you come in together several times. Where is she? I hope she isn't unwell.'

Now, this was awkward, she thought as she hadn't prepared an answer. Why is he so interested in Judy?

'To be honest, I don't know,' she replied. 'She just left without saying anything and I wonder if she is cross with me for some reason. I hope not. It will be difficult for me to get to work if she does not bring me in.'

Reuben ignored the hint and continued to ask about Judy. 'Maybe she has gone out with her boyfriend. Does she have a boyfriend?'

Christine laughed. 'Boyfriend. She will not let a man get within a metre of her. Between you and me, I think she has problems socializing. Sometimes she makes my friends feel quite uncomfortable, but I suppose I am used to her funny ways now.'

59

'I'm sure you are misunderstanding her,' he said, sounding annoyed. 'I have always found her extremely friendly in the staff room. She has a very gentle nature so I cannot imagine her being antisocial. It's just that she is a bit more reserved than some people.

Christine was also annoyed; annoyed that this young, attractive man had a good opinion of Judy, and, to make it worse, seemed to be comparing her own ways so negatively. Was he accusing her of being forward? What a nerve! Did he honestly think she would be interested in a weirdo like him? However, she knew she had to change her tone if she had any chance of getting another lift from Reuben.

'Oh, I didn't mean anything horrible about her. We are good friends it's just that she never seems interested in talking to men when we go out. I worry about her being so alone as I don't think it is a happy way to live her life.'

Reuben was no longer listening to her. His eyes were on the road ahead, but he was deep in thought. He didn't like Christine one bit and he made up his mind that he would not give her any more lifts, even to the bus stop.

Christine jumped out of the car quickly when they arrived at the house as she could sense his growing hostility and didn't want to give him the chance to ask for the bus fare after all. Despite his annoyance, Reuben waited until she had gone inside before driving away. At least he had got to see where Judy lived.

When he got home, Reuben saw his mother standing at the open front door, looking up and down the street as if it would hasten his arrival.

'Where have you been?' the woman yelled at him as he got out of the car.

He knew the neighbours would hear her but refused to be embarrassed. After all, everyone around there knew what she was like. 'I gave someone a lift home. Don't worry Mum, it was just a one-off,' he said, as she hugged him.

'Who was it? You didn't pick up a hitchhiker, did you? You know how much I worry about you driving at night.'

'You need to stop worrying. I would never be so stupid as to give a lift to a stranger. You've warned me enough times.' Reuben had given up reminding his mother that behind the genteel persona was a strong young man capable of holding his own in any fair fight.

'Then who was it? Was it a girl? Are you going to leave me, Reuben? I don't know what I'll do if you ever leave me.'

'I'll always come back.' He was sure she was getting more and more paranoid each time he left the house. 'I'll never leave you; I promise.'

Glasgow, June 1939

Eveline told James about the letter she had received from her sister, Bertha. He knew little about his wife's past, only that it wasn't a happy one, just like his own. One of the few details he did know was that she had spent a short part of her childhood in an orphanage, and she had only volunteered that information as it was required by the marriage registrar. She had no feelings of nostalgia towards her earlier life, and seldom, if ever, mentioned it. They were both forward-thinking people and their mutual desire to improve their lives had been part of the attraction between them.

After the end of the war the new decade had rolled in with a bang, bringing with it hope and optimism for those who had survived the horrors of the past years. However, despite being married for over fifteen years, they had no children, no friends, and Eveline rarely, if ever, left the tenement block they lived in. She had lost the optimism of her youth and was now merely existing. Her dark brown eyes had once danced in the light, yet now they were lustreless. It broke his heart.

He told her it would be a good thing to reconnect with her sister and maybe, one day soon, she could even visit her in London. It would give her something to look forward to again. So, a week after receiving the letter, Eveline sat down with a writing pad and pen, deciding not to burden her long-lost sister with her woes.

Chapter Eight

It was Judy's birthday and she had decided to buy something nice with the money that she wouldn't be spending on a night out with Christine. There was clearly not going to be a birthday drink. The two women had hardly spoken to each other since that drive home from college the day before when Christine had made it clear that she wasn't willing to spare a couple of hours of her free time for Judy's benefit. Well, she wouldn't let that stop her from marking the occasion herself.

Judy had thought about an evening out by herself - the cinema, the theatre, or a spa - but she didn't enjoy films, plays, or beauty treatments so in the end, she decided to buy something material which she could keep forever. She had not yet reached the time in her life where she could appreciate the value of a clock or an ornament, so only one thing remained. It was something that no one else was likely to buy her.

In the tiny jewellers she had felt a little embarrassed to be buying herself jewellery and she even considered pretending it was for someone else, a fictitious twin sister with the exact finger, wrist, and neck measurements. Somehow she just knew they wouldn't believe her. An attractive man was looking at the stone rings, probably for a surprise engagement, and she brooded for a moment over the possibility of any man asking her to marry him. Even as a teenager she believed any romance in her lifetime would not be the conventional relationship that most women enjoy.

A lump rose in her throat as she focussed on the silver section. Her thoughts wandered back to the St Christopher necklace and the charm bracelet that she kept in the musical jewellery box given to her by the grandmother she barely remembered. Why didn't she still have them, she wondered?

In the end she bought a gold and onyx bracelet which complemented her delicate wrist. It cost seventy pounds, far more than she had intended to spend. Nevertheless, it was a special birthday, regardless of what Christine thought. Pleased with her purchase she decided to cut short her day out and began to make her way home, without the visit to Littlewoods. The restaurant in Littlewoods reduced the price of their meals after four o'clock and she often took advantage when she didn't fancy a microwave meal. On her birthday, however, she fancied something a bit fresher. A Chinese, maybe. There was a takeaway on the route home.

She had quite a walk to her parked car and the rain wouldn't hold off much longer, so she stepped up the pace and was soon striding along the semi-residential streets that were made up of flats above shops. This was not a commuter area so there were very few people about, except for one person in front who seemed to be taking his time. When she got closer to him, she could see why.

The tall lanky figure was walking in an unnaturally straight line, as though being tested by traffic police, and trying hard not to stumble. She could tell it was Gary - the same leather jacket, the same dark jeans, and the dark curly hair that fell onto the back of his neck. Was it too late to turn around, she wondered? Yet if he also turned around and saw her walking away, it would be obvious she was trying to avoid him. After all, he would know that she hadn't passed him. Maybe she could walk past him quickly as if she didn't know it was him. He was clearly drunk and distracted by his attempt to stay upright. One thing was certain, she couldn't keep going at such an unnaturally slow place as it would look as if she were stalking him. Then it was too late. Suddenly, as though he could hear the various options churning around in her head, he stopped dead in his tracks.

Oh well, she decided, here goes. 'Hi, Gary. I wasn't sure if it was you or not as you were too far ahead. How are things?' she asked, with a cheeriness she didn't feel.

Gary had been walking with his face down to the ground and he was now standing in the same position only turned towards her. Slowly he raised his head and glanced at her briefly before looking downwards once again. He put his hands in the front pockets of his jeans then, leaning against a shop window, he squinted as if he was racking his brain for the words to give a response.

'Are you seeing Christine today?'

'Right, yeah,' he slurred. 'Chris's friend yeah? Er...'

'Judy.' Now she wished that she had just walked past him as clearly he would not have noticed her. Instead, she was now forced to have a conversation with him, drunk as he was.

'Hi Judy,' he said, with a slight grin. His expression lit up as if an idea had just come into his head. 'Where are you off to? You're not driving, are you 'cos, if you are, I could do with a lift? Been for birthday drinks with a few mates and I'm struggling, to be honest with you. What about it?'

Not on your life, she thought to herself, trying desperately to think of a reason why she wouldn't have her car with her. She never went anywhere without it, and he probably knew that too. Or did he? 'Er, well, I haven't finished shopping yet, so I won't be going to the car for a while.'

'You're not scared of giving me a lift, are you?' he asked, with a grin.

Judy hoped her cheeks weren't betraying the rising temperature that was burning inside her. 'No, of course not. Why on earth would I be scared of you?' she remarked, too quickly.

'Actually,' he replied. 'I meant scared to give me a lift cos I'm seeing Chris. I didn't think you were frightened of me. You're not, are you?' Again, a slight grin.

This was becoming so embarrassing it was making her forget her initial reluctance to have him in her car. 'Yes, of course I'll give you a lift. I suppose most of the shops are closing now and I was just killing time.'

'Cool. If it's alright with you, I'll wait here while you get the car. I can barely walk so I might have a little nap.'

Judy watched as he crouched down and placed his head on his crossed arms and wondered if he would still be there when she got back with the car. Hopefully, he would wake up and forget all about this unfortunate meeting, just as he had forgotten who she was when they had first spoken.

But that was not to be. Gary was standing up waiting as she turned the car onto the street that she had left him on. He clearly didn't know her car as he was still looking back and forth even as she approached him. So much for knowing she drove everywhere. Had he even known that she had a car when he asked if she was driving, or had he just been hoping? It was too late now so she sounded the horn, and he raised his hand in acknowledgement as he walked towards her, all the better for his brief nap.

She braced herself as he opened the passenger door and slid into a space that was too compact for his height. Despite any discomfort he did not attempt to move the seat back, instead just opened his legs so wide apart that he spread himself into the driver's space. Judy's hand brushed against his right leg as she put the car into first gear, and he moved it ever so slightly. This journey was going to be a challenge and it hadn't even begun.

'I don't know where you live, Gary,' Judy remarked, adding his name to distract from the pure awkwardness of the situation. It did not work.

'There is absolutely no need to worry about that. I can come back with you and wait for Chris there, which will save me coming over later. That's if you don't mind, Judy,' Gary replied, mimicking her gesture. With a complete lack of inhibition, he turned to look at her while she drove down the street. 'I didn't know you wore glasses,' he commented.

Why would you know I wear glasses, she thought to herself, grimacing? You didn't even know my name. 'I only use them for driving. You wouldn't want to be in this car with me if I wasn't wearing them.'

'I have no problem being in this car with you, Judy, and I have no problem with you wearing glasses. In fact, they look good on you.'

Judy grimaced once more. She had decided to give Gary a lift just to bring their meeting to an end, but the encounter was getting worse by the minute. And it wouldn't even be over when she got home because he was coming in the house too. What would she do if it was still just the two of them? If only she had turned around and walked away when she had the chance.

She turned on the radio to soften the silence that had filled the small intimate space they sat in, and she was glad to hear rock music blaring through the speakers, rather than the classical music she usually listened to. It worked as Gary was persuaded to sing along to the loud tune that Judy had never heard before. She tensed up when he placed his right hand on his knee which was already too close to her for comfort, and her eyes kept glancing down at his long fingers strumming to the guitar riff of the song. It was clearly a favourite of his. The music ended and she felt Gary's attention move back to her. She knew she was blushing.

'You like music, Gary?' she said, to distract him from looking at her, an obvious habit which was making her extremely nervous.

'Yeah. I play that song when I'm busking. It's a crowd puller.'

'Oh. I didn't know that you busked. Christine never mentioned it.' Judy sounded genuinely impressed. 'So, is it the guitar that you play? I noticed you strumming along to the music,' she said.

But he didn't answer. He was smirking.

She castigated herself for letting him know that she had been watching his hands while she was driving, and once again, she was blushing. But the drive was at last over. Now they just had to get through the time it took for Christine to return home from work. Luckily, as the car pulled up outside the house, she could see that Christine was letting herself in and it was no longer just the two of them. Thank heavens for small mercies.

When Christine looked up and noticed Gary in Judy's car she frowned. After she watched them getting out of the car, she walked over towards them. It was not something she was expecting to see. Then, with a smile which did not reach her dark brown eyes, she greeted Gary and Judy and said,

'What a surprise! I thought you weren't coming till tonight. How come both of you -?' before she was cut off by Gary who had moved away from Judy.

'Julie saw me sleeping in a doorway after too many pints and took pity on me. I was about to freeze to death,' he said, with another of those glances at Judy.

Christine threw her arms around him, giving him a long, lingering kiss. 'Well, I've got just the thing to warm you up.' She took his hand and led him down the hallway towards the living room.

As he closed the door behind him Judy caught his eyes glimpse towards her once more before disappearing behind the dark wood. That must be a habit of his, she thought.

Glasgow, June 1939

Dear Bertha,

How wonderful it was to read your letter. I have often thought about you these past years, always intending to search for you, but time is so hard to keep up with. You should be proud of yourself for everything you have achieved under such difficult circumstances. It is good to hear that you are married and have a home with Edward. Your little house sounds a lot bigger than ours, but, as there are only the two of us, it is big enough.

You were still a young child when I went into service, so I wonder if you remember what I look like. I have enclosed a photograph of James and I at our wedding. It was only a small affair with a few workers from Haworth as our guests. Forgive me for not sending you an invite but no outsiders were permitted to stay in our lodgings. Although we moved away not long after, our employers were extremely generous, giving James an excellent reference so that he found work rather easily.

We chose Glasgow because there was a lot of construction work happening here and James has good building skills. People come from all over the country to work here. Unfortunately, there are not enough jobs to go around all the men, so money is usually tight. If we can pay our rent and eat, I am more than satisfied as I don't need to buy clothes or go to the cinema, unlike James, who loves the American films. I am happiest staying at home.

It would be wonderful to see you and Edward. Of course, you could stay with us if you came up to Scotland, but you may find the conditions here a little cramped. There are many reasonably priced boarding houses near us which I think you would be more comfortable in.

Please write again soon and let me know when you will be able to visit.

Yours with love,

Eveline

Chapter Nine

Judy spent the next couple of hours in her room, deciding not to play gooseberry for once. So, this was going to be the rest of the evening, hiding in her bedroom with nothing to eat or drink. She felt more miserable than ever. Besides having nothing to do, she was hungry having chosen not to spend any money on eating out while shopping earlier, not even a cheese pasty. Nor did she pick up that Chinese takeaway due to Gary being in the car. Would he have wanted one too? Imagine what Christine would have thought about that.

There was no way she would try to grab some food while it sounded as if Christine had taken over the entire kitchen. Giving Gary a lift had also prevented her calling at the supermarket so there wasn't much to eat anyway. Yes, Gary had a lot to answer for. Even the gold bracelet that had filled her with joy earlier in the day, now hung limply on her wrist, looking as dull as her birthday was turning out to be.

She could hear the clattering of saucepans and the sound of the oven being lit, a bottle of something being opened, and feminine laughter. If only she had somewhere else to go, just for a few hours. Then she remembered Becky. Immediately, she rummaged in her handbag for the scrap of paper on which Becky's phone number was written, relieved that the telephone was in the hallway so she would not have to risk more humiliation if Becky was not in.

Becky was in but she was on her way out.

'Hi, Becky. It's Judy. I wondered if you fancy a drink for my birthday. I can pick you up and drive you home later.'

'Oh, I'm sorry, Judy. I'm working a night shift at the care home tonight, more fool me. Maybe another night?'

'Don't worry,' Judy said quietly, thinking how much more humiliated she would be if the others could hear the phone call.

'Look, I don't start my shift for another hour so if you meet me at St Mary's, we can have a birthday cup of tea and I'm sure the cook will spare us a piece of cake.'

'I'll be there in ten minutes.'

Judy was overjoyed at the invitation even if it took her out of the house for just an hour. She could call in Macdonald's after seeing Becky and maybe stay there for another hour. Grabbing her bag and keys, she rushed out of the house before the others could see that she was still wearing her day clothes, therefore not going anywhere special. She didn't want them to think she was only going for a drive by herself.

The care home where Becky worked was an attractive detached house in the outskirts of London. Becky pulled up just in front of Judy and waved her into the long driveway behind her. Then, handing Judy a present as she got out of the car, she walked around the back. Inside the building there was the generic odour that every residential home possessed, whatever the workers did to personalize it. Judy kept reminding herself of the only other place to spend the next couple of hours.

There was no cake left, but Becky made them both a mug of coffee and they sat in the conservatory. Judy looked around at the high-backed armchairs, most of them empty, but a few occupied. An elderly woman, awkwardly slumped, gazed back at her with unseeing eyes. A child's beaker of tea and a bowl of pale pink blancmange lay on a plastic tray in front of her while a uniformed girl with equally vacant eyes pushed a spoonful of the blancmange into the older woman's mouth. Nearest to Judy a woman with shocking red hair and a skeletal frame was struggling to lift herself from her seat, using the small table in front of her as a crutch. Tea slopped from a cup into its saucer and spilt onto a tea plate of uneaten Battenburg cake. Another young girl rushed over to guide her out of the room before the table was turned over.

'Oh well. So much for your birthday drink,' Becky said, rolling her eyes. 'What a cow Christine is. If I were you, I wouldn't waste my time thinking about her, especially as it's your day. Isn't there anyone in work you could ask?'

Just as Judy was about to explain that there wasn't, a care assistant walked over to Becky and talked quietly in her ear.

'I'm sorry but we've only got about ten minutes as I need to carry out an enema on one of the residents. Believe me, you wouldn't want to be around me after.'

Judy didn't know what an enema was and thought better than to ask. 'Oh, don't worry. I'm quite hungry so I'll nip to Macdonald's for an hour.'

'Who are you?' A brittle voice cut through their private conversation. A third resident, hitherto unnoticed by Judy, now demanded to know who she was. Most of the women at the home were lost in their own minds, a secret from everyone else, but this was one of the more extroverted residents and she refused to be ignored while an intruder was in her midst.

'You are naughty listening into private conversations, Iris.' Becky's voice had adopted the usual patronizing tone that her profession used when addressing elderly patients. 'Just sit there quietly for another ten minutes and everything will be back to normal.'

Judy felt bad for the older woman who was probably as lonely as she was, but Iris was not ready to be silenced.

'How dare you speak to me like that. I have every right to know who you bring into the house, and you can't tell me otherwise, or

Mr. Wells will give you your notice.' However, Becky had already left the conservatory at the sound of wailing from upstairs.

Judy was concerned at Iris's angry words. She didn't want to get Becky into trouble with her employer, so she tried to pacify the woman sitting near her.

'I'm sorry to disturb your evening. My name's Judy and it's my birthday today so I just popped in to collect my friend's present that she bought me.' She pointed to the gift bag at her feet. Her respectful tone had the desired effect and the woman nodded as if to accept her apology.

'Well, I suppose it makes a change to see a fresh face in the evening. How old are you, my dear?'

'I'm thirty.' Being in the presence of the aged woman, Judy almost felt guilty for her relative youth. However, that was until the woman spoke again.

'Thirty. Oh, I thought you were younger than that. What are you doing here on your birthday? Haven't you got a husband to take you somewhere special? I was married with three children by the time I was your age. My husband would not have married me if I had been thirty when we met. But people don't get married anymore, not like when I was young. They wait and wait in case something better comes along when really, things just get more difficult the older you are.' Her voice gradually reduced in volume as though she no longer wanted to be heard. Then the rhythmical stroking of a grandfather clock was all that broke the silence.

Judy looked down at her gold bracelet as she pondered the harsh words of the woman who was in the dying embers of her life. If Judy lived to that age, would she have three children to visit her? Probably not. Her death would likely be as lonely as her life. Then again, living a full life would make leaving it so much harder, when the end finally comes. How did that that Cat Stevens song go? Something about patches.

'She hasn't made you maudlin, has she?' Becky was back in the conservatory. 'Iris is one of our most depressing residents, always sees the downside in life.' She picked up the two mugs signalling the end of Judy's visit.

As they walked to the back entrance through which they had entered the home, Judy expressed her worry that Becky might get into trouble for allowing her into the conservatory.

'Will Mr. Wells be annoyed with you?' she asked Becky. That lady was quite angry when you practically told her to mind her own business.'

'I doubt it,' her now uniformed friend said laughing, 'He's been dead for over fifty years.'

Judy looked confused. 'But Iris said he would sack you or give you notice. Did you not hear her?'

'Mr. Wells was Iris's husband. He died in the war but now and again she forgets, just like she forgets she has outlived her children. All the ladies here are like that. One minute they are with you, as lucid as you and me, the next, away with the fairies. I don't know if it's a blessing or a curse.

In the sitting room Christine and Gary were eating the pasta dish she had made while pretending to watch television. It wasn't Christine's first choice to stay in as she had wanted to go to yet another party that Emma was having. One of the other tenants was moving out of the house and she didn't want to miss the opportunity of stating her interest in the soon-to-be-vacant room. Rather ironically, she knew her boyfriend hated socializing with other people, just as much as Judy. On the other hand, he was her boyfriend, and she was prepared to put up with his antisocial behaviour.

Gary had sobered up and was now in the mood for another lager, not tempted by the glass of Soave Christine had poured out for him. 'Why don't we nip to the Captain's Arms for a swift pint? It's only around the corner.'

He didn't sound hopeful, however, knowing how Christine liked the intimacy of the moment.

'I hate that place.' Christine snapped. 'Maybe you should take Judy. She's always trying to get me to go there too.' Then, a realization hit her, and she put her hand over her mouth. 'Oh no. It's her birthday today. I'd completely forgotten about it. I haven't even bought her a card, and it's her thirtieth, so she's probably feeling miserable enough as it is.'

Gary grinned. 'Thirty, eh. She's well left on the shelf, isn't she?'

The metaphor went over Christine's head, and she just looked at him blankly before continuing to regret her forgetfulness. 'If I hadn't already opened that bottle of wine, I could have pretended it was for her.'

'Why do you even care? You haven't spoken to each other for a few days and didn't even say hello when we were all at the door earlier.' Gary was genuinely confused at Christine's change of attitude.

Christine looked at him, wondering whether to try and explain her friendship with Judy. 'I know I say bad things about her sometimes, but I don't mean to fall out permanently. We just get on each other's nerves now and again. I meant to buy her something and I think I promised to go to the pub with her. It's just that I have been distracted – by you,' she admitted bashfully.

Gary saw his chance. 'Look, you can still go to the pub with her, I'll just come along too. You can pay for her drink and that'll be her present. If it helps, I'll sit at the bar on my own while the two of you make up.'

But Christine had no intention of spending the rest of the evening in that stinking place. If she agreed to go to the pub for a while, she and Gary could go to Emma's party after they had bought Judy her birthday drink. Judy could even go to the party with them if she wanted. However, Christine doubted that she would after the last party they went to together.

'Okay, but only if we can go to Emma's house after,' she said, ignoring his look of dismay. He couldn't have it both ways.

'Judy, are you there? Will you come to the pub with us to celebrate your birthday?' Silence. 'She must be asleep.'

Christine had knocked several times on the bedroom door and there had been no answer. 'Shall I open it? she asked Gary, who was standing near the front door.

He shrugged his shoulders. She turned the handle and poked her head around the door to find an empty room.

'She's not here. She must have gone out for food. We'll have to wait to see if she comes back.'

However, Gary was already halfway down the path, not willing to change this new direction of the evening.

'Hold on. I'll leave a note for her, saying we will be in the Captain's Arms until ten o'clock.'

After writing on a piece of paper she pushed it under Judy's door and then left with Gary.

London, September 1939

Bertha's fingers moved up and down the ivory notes slowly as she practised her scales and arpeggios. Although initially not interested in the piano, she found it helped calm her down whenever she got anxious, and right now, she was extremely anxious. She didn't understand why her husband was prepared to leave her all alone for the sake of the freedom of some country she had barely heard of. If what she heard about Poland was correct, it should be used to being occupied by another country.

They had gone through it all a year earlier with another obscure country's liberty tempting her husband away from her. That time it had all been a false alarm but not now. As a doctor, he might not have been called up for military service as people get sick in Britain, as well as France. If only she had married a coal miner or a dock worker because they might not have to go. Who would power the country if they did?

Her husband had claimed it was a matter of family honour, which made her accuse him of putting his blood family ahead of her. The last war had left her own father chronically sick and crippled, his poor wife all but a war widow for the short time they had before the flu finished them off. Bertha dreaded such a thing happening to her. She loved her husband, but she would rather him be killed than come back to her half the man he was.

'You could stay with my mother and father,' he had told her, as if somehow that would make the situation any better.

She hardly knew them, and they had not exactly welcomed her into the family. An East London orphan made good was how they saw her. They didn't understand that love sometimes traverses class boundaries. No. She would not be staying with them.

The day after he left, she moved into the middle room, not being able to bear the emptiness of their huge bedroom. The middle room faced the back of the house and, though not small, did not have the vast unused space of the front room. Indeed, the house itself was too big for their needs. Sometimes she envied her sister and James in their tiny tenement apartment unburdened by honourable family traditions.

Faced with even longer days at home alone she decided to offer her nursing skills voluntarily. There was sure to be a need at the hospital, especially if doctors were being killed abroad. Yes. She pulled down the lid of the piano and stood up. As soon as she had tidied the house, she would telephone the matron at the nearby hospital.

Chapter Ten

The rain battered the windscreen of the old Fiesta as the wipers fought a losing battle to keep it clear. Judy had missed the turn-off to McDonald's, unsure of the road markings, and now had to drive until she could turn around. She had been glad to leave the care home as the atmosphere had done nothing but depress her even more. It was difficult not to compare her life with the woman who had told her about having three children by the age of thirty. What did Judy have to show for her thirty years in the world? Nothing.

At least she had been given a present by someone other than herself, she thought, as she looked at the gift-bagged bottle of wine poking out from under her seat. When she got home later she would offer a glass to Christine and Gary which would show up Christine for the mean woman she was, not even getting a card for her. She grinned as she imagined Gary's opinion of his girlfriend change when he realized how spiteful she could be.

A car honked its horn at her as it was overtaking and she reprimanded herself for not concentrating more on her driving, especially in such horrible weather conditions. It was getting late, and the roads had quietened down after the familiar slog of the rush hour. However, the darkness, coupled with the faster speed of traffic, made the drive uncomfortably haphazard. She decided she would stop once she saw a side road just so she could get her bearings.

Unfortunately, to her horror she found herself on the motorway, not even sure in which direction she was heading. She was grateful that at least she was driving alongside, not towards, the other traffic. Cold comfort. To add to the misery a strong wind kept whipping the rain up from the ground, giving the impression of driving through deep water. To Judy's relief the lorry in front was now indicating left and she slowed down in anticipation of it disappearing down a slip road. Then she saw the sign for a service station, and she decided to keep behind it. At last, she could get off the road to have a cup of coffee and a sandwich.

The service station car park was large but almost empty, as the lorry had followed a different lane to the back of the paved area. Judy pulled up next to an old red Fiesta before seeing that it was full of teenagers smoking cigarettes or something stronger. They looked at her briefly as she switched off the ignition, then turned away again. She regretted not looking more closely at the car before she had pulled up next to it, but that was just a petty thing in the context of the evening. So she locked the car door and ran towards the comfort of the illuminated building.

To her dismay the service station café area was almost empty which was to be expected given the absence of cars in the car park. There was a group of people who looked like travellers, with several young children running around the foyer in an uncontrolled manner. The only other customer was a man sitting by himself, nursing an empty mug. This was not the anonymous setting in which she had hoped to eat.

Judy bought a coffee and sat down a few rows back from the solitary man, on the opposite side of the room. That way he was not able to watch her, she thought, at least until she saw her reflection in the window facing him which might just as well have been a mirror. And he was watching her, of course, as she was probably not a typical visitor at this time of the evening. She had no luggage with her, no workbag, no files. She did not even have a pen to doodle with. What must he be thinking? What if he thought she was a prostitute? The idea horrified her. Suddenly being back at the house with Christine and Gary didn't seem quite so bad, so she finished her coffee and left the café as quickly as she could.

The rain was now a light drizzle, and she was relieved that the drive home would be less of an ordeal. But there would be no drive home, not that evening anyway. As she approached her car the sight that met her took a few seconds to become meaningful. There was a brick on the driving seat which she could see through the large, jagged hole in the window. Glass lay everywhere inside. The car with the teenagers in had disappeared, and so had Judy's car radio. Her heart sank.

'I've called the police.'

The voice made Judy jump. Standing behind her was a security guard who was holding a dustpan and brush. 'They usually pop in about this time for a bite to eat.'

Judy looked puzzled for a second. The people who vandalized her car? Then she realized he was talking about the police.

'It was those kids you know, the ones you parked next to.' His tone was critical. 'I was trying to keep an eye on them, but they were too quick for me. I'll clear it up the best I can, and you should be alright to drive it now that the rain has stopped.'

Judy stood back while the security guard started to brush the broken glass into the pan. She didn't have the stomach to help him. If only she had moved her car closer to the entrance, she would be on her way home now. Instead, she had not wanted to look a fool in front of those thieving yobs. She certainly looked a fool now.

There was the sound of a car pulling up too close behind them, doors opening, then footsteps. A policewoman was now part of the audience viewing the security guard sweeping inside the battered car. Then she turned to look at Judy.

'Are you the owner of this vehicle?' she enquired, in a bored voice.

Even though she was speaking to Judy, the policewoman was looking past her at the entrance of the station towards which her colleague was heading. Judy nodded miserably. She gave a description of the teenagers and their car as best she could while hoping desperately that she wouldn't be asked to explain why she was there at such an odd time. But she reassured herself she wasn't the criminal. And the policewoman was not in the slightest bit interested in her beyond what had happened to her car. And she didn't seem much interested in that either.

'Are you comfortable driving without the window? If you leave now, the rain should hold off until you get home.' The policewoman placed her notebook in her back pocket and looked again in the direction of the entrance of the service station.

'Oh dear,' the security guard remarked suddenly.

The two women looked at him with curiosity. Then, holding the dustpan towards Judy, he pointed towards a wiry object nestled amongst the pieces of glass. That was it. The night had now reached its nadir, Judy thought. It could get no worse.

'My glasses,' she cried. 'I can't drive without them, especially in the dark. What am I going to do?'

For the first time the policewoman looked sympathetic. 'Is there someone you could call to pick you up?' she asked.

'No.' So now there was total humiliation. Judy was faced with having to explain herself. No friend. No boyfriend. No flatmate. Should she pretend that she had argued with a boyfriend or just tell the truth?

'Can I help in any way?'

It was the man from the café. How long had he been standing there, she wondered?

'I couldn't help overhearing,' he explained. 'I'm happy to give her a lift.' He was speaking directly to the policewoman as if Judy were a child.

'That's incredibly good of you sir,' she said, answering for Judy who had now abandoned all semblance of self-respect.

Then the security guard and policewoman arranged for the damaged car to be sheltered around the side in the motel car park.

They shared a joke before the policewoman finally journeyed towards her colleague indoors and the guard took the keys from Judy's hand. Before moving the car, he handed Judy the gift box containing the wine which had survived the earlier incident unscathed.

The metronome on top of the piano was ticking at sixty beats per minute as the woman kept in time perfectly. Reuben's mother was a natural and her mother had said she would be a famous concert pianist when she grew up. Of course, that did not happen as she stopped playing when her mother disappeared the night of the bombing. Her father wanted her to continue with the lessons, but her piano teacher had died the night of the bombing too.

For so many years the sound of piano notes, which she had previously loved, reminded her of the moment her world had nearly ended. Each tune brought back yet another painful memory that made her feel incredibly said. But then her son spent so much money on a new piano for her sixty-fifth birthday that she felt obliged to make the effort. Before long she found herself yearning to caress the notes once again.

Her favourite pieces were by Schubert, particularly his Serenades which brought a feeling of calm and lightness to her. But she never played those tunes in front of Reuben because he could never witness the tears that streamed down her face as the memories of that night returned.

Reuben loved to hear his mother play as it was a sign that she was still functioning in some way. He picked up one of the photographs on the mantlepiece to see a young woman staring back at him. It could have been his twin sister if it weren't for the age of the photograph. Although he had never met his grandmother, he knew how much he resembled her from the many black and white photographs that his mother had placed around the house. There was at least one photograph in every room. The photographs, she said, made her believe her mother was still there with her. Because she had to be somewhere.

'I thought you looked upset in the services,' said the man, while opening the passenger door of his car first. 'I was going to ask you if you needed any help but then you left quite suddenly. My name's Geoff, by the way. I didn't catch your name.'

'I'm Judy. I was more stressed than upset because the driving conditions were so bad. I fell out with my flatmate and wasn't ready to go home. I'm sure she's pulling her hair out, right now,' she lied.

'Flatmate, eh. It must have been a serious row to make you end up here,' he said, raising an eyebrow.

'Not exactly. I probably overreacted. People are always calling me over-sensitive,' she admitted, more to herself than the stranger. 'Besides, I fancied a drive because it gives me time to think.' If only she had thought before storming out of the house, she mused. 'It's really good of you to drive me back. I don't think that policewoman had much time for me. I seemed to be delaying her dinner.'

'Yes, I thought that too. Unfortunately, this is a hotspot for car crime, and they're probably called out several times a day over it, with no hope of catching them.' He realized what he had said and quickly changed the subject. 'So how will you get back to your car tomorrow?' he enquired, sounding concerned. 'Is there anyone who can give you a lift to the service station?'

He turned his head in time to see Judy scanning the footwells of the car, looking for evidence of a wife or children - sweet wrappers, hairbrush, makeup. There was nothing.

'Oh, I can get a taxi. I have to go to the opticians first in any case.'

'I can't believe they smashed your glasses. Little shits.' Somehow his words made Judy feel even more pathetic. Her eyes welled with tears which she hoped he couldn't see.

The journey took little more than fifteen minutes which made Judy realize how hopelessly lost she had been. She thought she had been driving for at least an hour. As they pulled up outside the house Judy peered through the rainy passenger window. She couldn't see a light through the frosted glass in the front door so Christine may have gone out somewhere. She wasn't sure which was the least appealing prospect - facing her again or facing the empty house.

'Is this really where you live?'

The rhetorical question did not help. 'It's fine actually. There is plenty of room and it's cheap and cheerful,' she lied again. 'There's no point in wasting money on a rented place.' She found herself glancing at the fourth finger of his left hand. It was bare.

'I didn't think anyone still lived around here. I bet it hasn't changed since the German air raids.'

For the first time, there was an uncomfortable silence.

'Er, thanks again for the lift. I hope your family won't be worried about you.'

'I live alone so they wouldn't know.' His tone was genial, yet it evoked a slight feeling of anxiety in Judy. 'Are you sure you don't want me to drive you back to your car tomorrow?'

'No. I can manage.'

'Well,' he said, unconvinced, 'here's my number in case you have any trouble getting back to your car. It's not going to be easy unless you have someone to give you a lift to the service station.'

Judy blushed with embarrassment as she took the business card from him. First, she had to get replacement driving glasses. Then somehow get to her car which was left at the service station. Being without her car had left her helpless and she was desperate to get back that small control of her life. She looked at the card he had given her and put it in her bag. Perhaps she should break with her own tradition and take up his offer of help. After all, that's what Christine would do. But then again she was nothing like Christine.

Glasgow, February 1940

Dear Bertha,

Thank you for James's birthday present. It was kind of you and Edward to go the effort of sending it. With the money we went to the pictures to see Gone with the Wind. James was so excited as we hadn't been to the pictures for such a long time. He loved the film, though I must confess I found it rather long.

I hope Edward is safe and well. This is a peculiar war and hopefully it will be over before it has begun. It is unfortunate that your husband has chosen to serve in the air force as they appear to be the only soldiers in action.

We were sad to hear that his father died, especially so soon after his mother. How cruel that he couldn't see them before they passed away. Is it right that he only has cousins left on his side of the family now? I don't suppose you will have much to do with them either. At least you both have a bit of security now though I understand it will be cold comfort for a while.

We have also suffered a little misfortune though not to the same extent. James fell off a ladder and broke his ankle while he was working at the building site. The company said it was his own fault as he should not have been up the ladder without it being held. They refused to accept that there were not enough workers to ensure such a safety measure. He will be unable to work for a while so there will be no more treats until he is better, but as long as we are all safe that is all I care about. Please be careful down there on your own.

Look forward to your next letter.

Yours with love,
Eveline

Chapter Eleven

Christine and Gary had just arrived at her friends' house party, but they were not in the party mood. It had been raining for the past fifteen minutes and neither was feeling sociable. They had waited at the pub for two hours, but Judy didn't turn up. By then Christine had just about had enough of the smell of smoke and stale beer plus the repetitive sound of pool balls slamming against hard wood. Gary, of course, would have happily stayed there until closing time so Christine had to virtually dragged him out of the pub door. He'd tried to persuade her to give up on the party and return to the house, but she wouldn't hear of it.

She thought the long walk would freshen them up before they got to her friend's house, but it would have been a better idea to get a taxi as it turned out. Her friend Emma directed them to the utility room where they could deposit their sodden outerwear. However, Gary was reluctant to leave his leather jacket there, and at first, insisted on keeping it on.

'What is wrong with you? No one will want to stand next to you if you are soaking wet,' Christine snapped, 'Take the wretched thing off, for heaven's sake. I'll meet you in the kitchen.'

Gary rolled his eyes and began to take off his jacket while she walked away to join her friends in the party. He hated house parties and would rather be in the pub where he could watch whatever football match might be on the pub television. It wasn't that he was a big drinker as he would happily stay at home practising his guitar riffs and writing lyrics. Small talk was not his thing and he had nothing in common with any of Christine's snooty friends. He had already drunk more than he wanted, and the punch wasn't going to tempt him. On the other hand, he knew that Christine was on the verge of a tantrum, so he gave in.

Before joining his girlfriend, he reached into the inside pocket of his jacket, removed the flick knife, and pushed it down into his front jean pocket. He would have to remember to put it back before they left, he thought. The last thing he needed was for Christine to feel it when she finally wanted some attention. However, it turned out there would be no need to wait that long.

'What's that?'

He looked up startled. Standing in the doorway was a suspicious-looking Christine, having seen him put the knife into his pocket. She wasn't sure exactly what it was but assumed it was something he didn't want anyone, even her, to know about. It explained the secrecy and reluctance to leave his jacket.

'What's what? What are you talking about?' he snarled defensively, but he could feel the colour rising in his neck. How long had she been standing there, he wondered?

'What did you just take out of your jacket pocket and put in your jean pocket when you thought I wouldn't see you?' Her voice cut through the warm damp air.

'Why do you want to know?' he retorted. 'Who do you think you are trying to catch me out? I don't spy on you.'

Christine glared at him suspiciously. 'It was a knife, wasn't it? You have a knife. Gary, why are you carrying a knife around with you?' She had believed it was drugs, not a knife, but thought he would be more likely to confess when faced with a worse accusation. His response was not what she had hoped it would be.

'I carry it for self-defence,' he said finally. 'There are a lot of bad people out there Christine. It's not so bad where you live, but there are all sorts of lowlife where I live. You could get murdered in your bed if they think you are defenceless. I've never used it though, honest.'

'So, you think you are not a lowlife yourself, walking around with a deadly weapon, and while I was with you too. I can't believe it. Get out. I don't want a criminal for a boyfriend. I never want to see you again.' she said, almost spitting at him.

Gary grabbed his jacket and pushed past her angrily. 'If that's what you think of me you can sod off.' He continued walking out through the front door and back into the evening rain.

Christine stood by herself in the small cold room, not knowing whether she was shaking from the cold or the shock of the last few minutes. Drugs she might have been able to handle, well, maybe Cannabis or that kind of thing, certainly nothing too illegal. Knives, however, were on another level. She knew from the way Gary had reacted that he was not telling the truth about the knife being for self-defence, and she couldn't bear to think what he really used it for. Mugging people? Robbing shops? There was nothing that could be acceptable. Whatever his reasons, she would have nothing more to do with him. Her standards in men were not exceptionally high, but they were certainly above violence.

The horizontal rain driving icy blows into his face increased Gary's irritation. Why did she think she had the right to see his personal possessions? It wasn't as if they had been going steady. They had only just met, well, not that long ago anyway. What would she think if he demanded to look through her handbag while she was watching him? She should have been grateful that he went to the damned party with her in the first place. At least he had been spared the guaranteed boredom if he had been allowed to stay.

As these thoughts were pounding through his head, he fumbled around with the knife that was back in his jacket pocket. Looking around him, he decided he might as well have a quick scan of the area while he was out, the rain keeping the dark streets empty. Gary loved walking the streets at night, confident that any other solitary man he saw was also up to no good and would keep away from him. The cars in this part of London were mostly old and battered which made them perfect targets for him. It was not his aim to steal the car after all, just take anything else he could flog, car phones, radios, even CDs.

Experience had taught him not to be greedy and he walked past the cars with the more expensive interiors, knowing they would cause him too much bother with their alarms and coded electrical fittings. Finally, he came across a car which he knew he could break into – an old Ford Fiesta without central locking and the alarms that go with it. He took out the knife and within seconds had opened the driver's side of the car and dismantled the radio, which was a good one. It was probably worth more than the car, he thought to himself. He might get about twenty quid for it. Just before leaving, he opened the glove compartment and noticed a large brown envelope. He took it out and felt it then after prising it open, he gasped. It was filled with wads of twenty-pound notes.

Gary could not believe his luck. His heart started to pound as he flicked through each wad to check the money was real. Suddenly he heard a yell coming from somewhere outside of the car and looked up to see a man running down the garden steps of a nearby house. He had to get out of there. Dropping the radio, he tucked the envelope of money into his inside jacket pocket and fled without looking back, the sounds of the pursuing steps getting fainter and fainter.

Gary was a fast runner and before long, confident he was safe, he looked again at the money – a mixture of twenty- and fifty-pound notes which were all used. There must have been ten thousand pounds in the envelope, drug money he was sure, so he knew it would be wise for him to keep a low profile for a while. He knew exactly what he would spend the money on. If he bought a van, an amplifier, and a decent guitar he was sure he could get himself enough gigs to pack in that braindead factory job. Would Christine turn her nose up at him then, he wondered? But that was in the future. For now, he had to get clear of any danger. Aware that the man he had stolen the money from would probably be searching for him in his car, he didn't want to walk all the way home, so he decided to take a chance on calling somewhere nearer.

At the party Christine was feeling self-conscious for the first time in a long while. Everyone there she knew was cuddled up with their mate and those that she didn't know looked happy in the various groups they had formed. Probably due to her miserable mood, nobody seemed to be interested in her joining them and who could blame them. This must be how Judy feels, she thought to herself, wishing that Judy was with her now. If only they had waited for her to come back from wherever she was before leaving for the pub. That was Gary's fault for being too impatient. After all, Judy couldn't have gone any further than the local shop as she didn't know anyone but Christine.

Guilty thoughts raced through her mind as she remembered how hostile she had been to the idea of spending money on a meal for Judy's birthday. Now, she would have to spend a fortune on a taxi to get home. But it would be worth it to put an end to a disastrous night. She looked around for Emma and found her in the middle of a closed circle of partygoers. Christine pushed her way into it. As usual, Emma was the centre of attention but when she saw Christine, she turned to face her.

'Are you okay, Christine? Where's Gary? I haven't seen him since you arrived. Why are you on your own?'

'He's gone and he won't be back,' Christine replied, determined not to show she was upset; she had no intention of discussing her reasons with anyone. What would they think of her if they knew she had dated a man who carried a knife? No. She would keep that bit of information to herself. 'I don't know anyone here, Emma. Maybe I should get a taxi home.'

'Oh, I'm so sorry, and I thought you were such a good match. Please don't go, Christine. You've only just arrived, and you haven't had any of my punch. I'll find you someone decent to talk to, and you can stay here tonight. Don't waste your money on a taxi.'

For once, Christine would have preferred to give up on the party and call time on her rotten evening, at least then she could find out what had happened to Judy. Then again, what if Gary came back to the party and she had already left. He might be drunk and cause a scene, then everyone would know what had happened. If he came back while she was still there, she could take him away from the party so he wouldn't embarrass her. So, despite her misery, she decided to stick it out at the party.

True to her word Emma led Christine over to a young man sitting on his own and introduced them to each other. 'Christine, this is Tristen. Tristen works at the job centre with Tim. Tristen, this is Christine. She's envying that settee. Is there room for her?'

Tristen was handsome if a little dull, and Christine wasn't really in the mood for flirting. But realizing that he was gay, she was more than willing to spend the next couple of hours pinned to his side. At least she was no longer by herself. He wasn't too demanding in the way of conversation, so it gave her a chance to reminisce about the time she and Gary had caught each other's eye that first night they were in the pub. It had been her that he had given his attention to, not her friends, and there was sensation of a spark lighting between them. They had even talked about him joining her in France over the holidays. Well, that spark was extinguished as soon as she saw his knife. It would take three weeks away to recover from the horrible experience. Trying not to cry, she turned to the man sitting next to her and asked him to refill her glass.

Silence met Judy when she entered the hallway, and something told her the house was empty. Despite her earlier feelings, she was disappointed. She had hoped Christine would be in when she got back home just to return to some semblance of normality. Had they gone out shortly after she had? If only she had waited a bit longer before phoning Becky the evening would not have turned into such a nightmare. Too late now. There was no light in the hall as the bulb had died and was too high to replace. For a moment she stood in the darkness and listened out for unfamiliar sounds, but there was only silence, so she eased her way into the kitchen.

As she was filling the kettle, she wondered if a cup of tea would cure all the ills that she had encountered that day. But she knew it was just an old wife's tale. Taking the milk out of the fridge, she remembered the bottle of wine that Becky had given her for her birthday. It was still in the gift bag she had thrown onto the settee, and taking it out, she was pleased to find that it was quite an expensive bottle. Becky did not buy anything cheap.

Judy didn't usually drink white wine, but at this moment in time, it seemed far more appealing than tea. Now to find a corkscrew she thought, opening each drawer more in hope than expectation. No corkscrew should mean no wine. Normally she wouldn't risk a cork-filled glass of wine which was always the result of her trying to remove it without the necessary corkscrew. Nevertheless, tonight was an exceptional situation, and she pulled a wooden spoon out of one of the drawers, sat herself down on the settee with the bottle between her knees, and began to push the spoon handle down on the cork. After a few unsuccessful minutes she gave up on the spoon and removed a vegetable knife, intending to cut the cork out in pieces. The knife looked very sharp, and it was at that point that the idea of just going to bed entered her head, but she persevered for another five minutes. Then there was a gentle knock on the front door.

London, March 1940

Volunteering at the hospital made Bertha feel as though she had a purpose in life beyond that of being a wife and, God-willing, a mother. There had been little need for her so far, but it allowed her to refresh her medical skills. She had also started giving piano lessons to some of the local children for free. It was not her idea, but once again, her husband's. He thought it was a way of contributing to the war effort, or the Phoney war as she had heard people call it.

Edward would be coming home on leave soon and she wasn't going to tell him about her work at the hospital. He would be sure to disapprove even though it was far more useful than risking one's life dropping endless pieces of paper over a foreign country. What sort of war was this anyway? Yet he would be adamant she should stay at home, especially after the legacy he got from his parents which further removed the need for her to earn a wage. But she wasn't interested in the money, just the reward she got from being useful to other people, people who couldn't otherwise manage.

It had given her great satisfaction to hear that Eveline's husband had loved his trip to the cinema, the trip that she had paid for. Now that James was unable to work, Bertha decided to send money more regularly to help them make ends meet. There was plenty of money to spare and Edward would be more than happy if Bertha spent it on expensive clothes and jewellery. Perhaps he married the wrong woman. Sometimes it made Bertha mad to think that, if she hadn't married Edward, she would not have had to give up her job, a job she loved, for the sake of sitting in that damned house day after day.

Chapter Twelve

Judy looked at her watch. It was eleven o'clock so who could possibly be calling around this late? Christine had a key and would have called out to announce herself. Surely it wasn't that Geoff guy as he had just dropped her off. Had she left something in his car, she wondered? Or perhaps he was a bit of a creep. She walked towards the door and looked through the frosted glass before a familiar voice called out,

'It's me, Gary. Sorry to call by so late.'

Judy opened the door slowly to see Christine's boyfriend looking drenched and uncharacteristically sheepish as well as being out of breath. He glanced down at her hand and frowned. She was still holding the knife.

'Oh, er, I wasn't able to find a corkscrew and I couldn't push it down,' Judy explained, realizing she must have looked like a paranoid woman, too scared to answer the door without a knife.

Gary rolled his eyes in an expression of mock exasperation. 'Give it here,' he said, resuming his familiar air of arrogance and he marched past her, leaving her to close the door behind him. He saw the wine on the floor surrounded by bits of cork. 'Are you celebrating something?' he asked, raising his eyebrows. He wondered if someone else was in the house. Had Christine come home early? If she had, she must be really upset. On the other hand, if she had stayed at the party, she clearly didn't care that much about their split.

'No. I don't usually drink in the house, but I've had a bit of a rotten day,' she said, hoping that he wouldn't ask her about it. But he obviously had no interest in the answer to his own question and had already forgotten it was her birthday. By the time Judy had finished her sentence, he had already taken the bottle out into the kitchen, and a few seconds later she heard the cork pop. Then cupboard doors were opened and closed, and she heard the unmistakeable sound of wine being poured.

'Here you are,' he said, holding a cup towards her. I couldn't find a glass for you but I'm sure it tastes just as good in a cup.'

Judy took the cup and looked at the contents. There was no sign of any cork, just the greenish-yellow wine still swirling around at the bottom of the cup. She took a sip, then another. It was what she needed at that moment.

'Would you like a glass; I mean a cup?' she said, with a giggle that surprised both. 'And Christine, of course,' she added quickly. She hadn't noticed that he was unaccompanied and thought Christine could have been chatting to friends in a shared taxi.

'Cheers,' he said, and poured himself a drink. 'Christine's not here. She's gone to a party with her mates, and I didn't fancy it.' He sat down on one of the kitchen chairs and took a large gulp of wine, pulling an unimpressed face. He didn't want to go back outside for at least another few hours so after taking off his wet jacket he began to turn on the charm. 'The thing is, we had an argument. She was asking too much of me. It's not as if we've been going out that long and she wants to know my every move. I'm not ready to be that kind of boyfriend yet.'

'Oh, I'm sorry,' said Judy while wondering why he had turned up at the house if he had no intention of making up with Christine. Her heart began beating faster and her legs felt weak making her sway slightly.

Gary was watching Judy closely and he pulled out another chair. 'Why don't you sit down too? A lady shouldn't stand while a man is sitting down comfortably, especially when there's wine in the room.' He paused for a few seconds before adding with raised eyebrows, 'We haven't had a chance to get to know each other, have we?'

Judy poured herself some more wine then sat down next to Gary, wondering what he was thinking at that moment. He had flirted with her before, but never in a situation in which they would remain alone together for some time. She was certainly not looking her best after the drama of the service station, but she never really made much effort in the way of clothes and makeup. Moreover, Christine was far from a beauty queen.

'I get the feeling that you two don't get on that well,' he said, as if he didn't already have an idea from being with Christine. 'So how come you keep sharing a house when you don't seem to be able to sit in the same room.' It was a fair question and Judy wondered how to answer it.

'We were, I mean we are friends, but, when you live together and work together it gets a bit much sometimes.' Judy wondered if she meant it. They had had some good times together. It couldn't all be Christine's fault, could it? But then she remembered that Christine had not even bought her a birthday card.

'You always look so sad,' he said suddenly.

'I suppose it's because it's my thirtieth birthday and I've spent it by myself," she replied, not caring how pathetic she sounded to herself.

'I think you need a man to give you a big birthday hug.' He was grinning as though he was talking about a nameless man who wasn't him, which took away some of the intimate nature of the comment.

Judy laughed and said, 'If only I could get him on prescription.'

Gary was staring at her now and she could feel herself tingling. She stood up again and walked over to the bottle of wine, putting her hands on the worktop to steady herself. There was a long, awkward silence before she heard him get up too. Then he was standing directly behind her so she could feel his breath on her neck. Her heart was beating so fast the rest of her body didn't have a chance to gather oxygen and she turned to face him. She held one of his hands and caressed his long fingers.

'You have a musician's hand. I'd love to hear you playing the guitar, Gary.' She looked into his eyes for only a few seconds before she closed hers and opened her lips to meet his. A few minutes passed and he leant back, his eyes fixed on hers, both lost in the moment, and forgetting about anyone else.

'I think we should go to your room, Judy' he said, tilting his head slightly.

And that was where they went.

Several hours later Judy lay with her head in the crook of Gary's arm. For the first time she could remember, she was blissfully happy. This handsome man had made love to her just as was happening to thousands of other women her age, and it had been beautiful, not seedy. She could feel normal, for now anyway. She felt him beginning to awake from his slumber and wondered what was going to happen next. She pretended to be asleep as she felt his head turn towards her, then he turned away, moving her head away from him at the same time. His body which she had been part of just a few hours ago was now stiff and cold. It was time for her to wake up from her pretend sleep.

He got dressed quickly and left the room and she heard him run up the stairs into the bathroom. He reappeared a few minutes later and sat on the bed to put his trainers on.

'Hello,' she said softly, but he kept his back to her while he spoke, 'This should not have happened. I'm sorry.' Within a minute he had picked up his jacket and once again walked out of the bedroom door.

'Gary, wait,' she shouted, wrapping her dressing gown around her quickly, but he had already left the house.

Although tired and hungover, Judy knew she didn't have any time to waste on her own recovery as she had to retrieve her car.

However, the events of the night before had thrown her into emotional turmoil, and she needed to talk to somebody. The only person she could think of was Becky and, just as she'd done the previous evening, she rang her.

'Hi, Becky. Sorry, did I wake you? You never guess what happened to me last night?'

Becky had just got home from her night shift and was ready to crash but, hearing the excitement in Judy's voice, her curiosity was piqued. 'Judy, what's happened. Did you get home alright? I hope you enjoyed that bottle of wine,' she said, playfully.

Judy didn't have much change, and her experience at the service station wasn't a priority so she quickly told Becky how she'd slept with Christine's boyfriend and how he had turned cold on her in the morning. She could hear the gasps of surprise and laughter coming down the phone and was glad that Becky had found the funny side of it. Some people may have been disapproving of what she and Gary had done but Becky had heard enough about Christine to dislike her, even without knowing her personally.

Trust you,' she said. 'What about Madame? Are you going to tell her?'

No. She's got a bit of a temper so I can't be sure she wouldn't kill me. If I'm not here when you call next, you know what's happened to me,' Judy said, jokingly.

The pips went and Becky shouted that she would call Judy in a few days to arrange to meet up. Although Gary had gone cold on her, it didn't matter to Judy. At last, she had something to talk about, something exciting that had happened to her. Christine could be as smug as she wanted but it wouldn't bother her anymore. Judy might have felt guilty if it hadn't been for Christine ignoring her birthday, but not now.

Gary ran down the street, away from the night before. He pulled his collar up as if it would help conceal his identity from hostile onlookers. Thinking about Christine finding out and if she would ever forgive him, he wondered if he could just deny everything. Unfortunately, that tactic hadn't worked well when trying to explain the knife. He was ashamed of sleeping with Judy; however, it was something he had to do at that time. Hopefully, she wouldn't tell Christine as he had given her the cold shoulder making it obvious it wouldn't happen again.

She had been worryingly soppy when he woke up, so it was best to nip things in the bud. He really was fond of Christine and was willing to reform if she would give him another chance, but it would be difficult to speak to her before she left for France. Perhaps it was best to give her enough time to miss him.

Just as he was about to turn into the park he felt in his pocket and took out a packet of cigarettes and a lighter; something else he would have to give up, he thought. Running had made him hot, and he took off his jacket and held it in one hand. The streets had been almost deserted when he left the house, but the rush hour traffic was already building up as he walked away from the centre towards the area of his own house. Cars were being driven in the direction he walked away from, becoming slower as time passed, and the numbers increased. Joggers confronted him from either behind or in front, some swearing as they inhaled the smoke from Gary's cigarette, some deliberately pushing into him as they passed. He turned towards a park entrance where he thought the joggers should be instead of bothering pedestrians.

Inside the park, it was much quieter. A few committed dogwalkers gathered in the middle of the football pitch, engrossed in canine discussion while watching a motley group of dogs play fighting and chasing each other. A black and white whippet was running around in large circles, gradually getting close to the edge of the field, causing its owner to call out. Suddenly, Gary felt conspicuous with neither a dog nor a jogging kit. He supposed that he looked quite threatening to the elderly woman walking her two miniature dogs ahead of him, so he veered off the path into the shelter of some bare trees. That was the moment his pursuer took their opportunity. Gary knew instantly that he had been stabbed, and before he could turn to face his assailant, he collapsed to the ground.

London, April 1940

Bertha was standing at the top of the stairs, staring at the small stained-glass window in the back wall. When they had first bought the house, she and Edward loved its ornateness and its boldness; the tiny yellow, blue, and green panes surrounding the stark centrepiece of the bird. She imagined the raven sitting on the branch of a tree in full bloom on a late summer's day. Despite its harsh features, devilish colour, and rasping calls, it could sit as proudly on that branch as the beloved blackbird.

However, now all she saw were the eyes of the raven judging her each time she walked past it. It was as though Edward could still see her. Were its beady eyes warning her of dark times ahead? What began as her imagination was turning into a real feeling of foreboding, so she decided to be rid of it. She would hire a man to cover it with plywood then plaster over it. After all, it was unlucky to have birds in the house.

Chapter Thirteen

Having slept little the night before, Judy was showered and dressed by seven o'clock and bracing herself for the day ahead. If only she had kept her old glasses as a spare pair. Then she could have gone directly to the service station, driven to a glazier to fix the window, and got to college by ten for her first class of the day. But, of course, she didn't have a spare pair and she ended up sitting in the optician for over an hour. And it hadn't opened until nine o'clock. She missed her college class which added to the financial cost of the whole miserable experience and had ended up with the most unflattering pair of glasses she had ever seen. The elation from the previous night's passion was already becoming a distant memory.

Just as she was approaching a taxi to take her to her car, she realized that in all the drama of the previous evening she had failed to make a mental note of the service station that she had driven to. She rarely drove outside of London so one service station was much like another as far as she was concerned. There was nothing else for it. She would have to ring Geoff if only to ask him the name of the service station. He would think she was an idiot for not knowing where she had driven to, but he probably thought that anyway. She picked out his card, lost amongst the old pieces of paper in her handbag, and reluctantly dialled the number.

'Hi, Judy. You just caught me.' Geoff sounded different from the night before. More distant.

'Er… I know this sounds stupid but I'm not sure how to get to the service station. Which junction was it?' Was that someone's voice in the background? A woman's voice.

'I can be with you within the hour.'

'It's okay. I just need the junction. I'm not at home anyway.'

'I'm not sure. Sorry.'

'That's alright. Sorry to bother you.' She hung up. That was the second time in a couple of hours that a man had turned cold on her. Men could be so weird.

'Is everything okay between you and Christine now?'

Judy was taken aback by Reuben's question which was both personal and seemingly intuitive. Up until that moment they had been sharing small talk while queuing for the photocopier but once they were alone, he had immediately changed the topic of conversation.

Aware of her confused look, he quickly added, 'I hope you don't mind me asking but she told me you had fallen out when I gave her a lift home yesterday. It must be difficult to house share when you are not speaking.'

'I suppose she asked you for a lift,' Judy replied, shaking her head. 'I can't believe the gall of that woman.'

'She's certainly not backwards in coming forwards,' Reuben said, with just a little more diplomacy. He didn't want to give Judy the impression that he had given much thought to Christine. 'Does that mean that you haven't reconciled your differences?'

Judy was about to comment on the use of the word 'differences' but thought better of it. She didn't know Reuben that well so she shouldn't really discuss her relationship with Christine too much. She decided to change the subject once again and told him what had happened to her car and how she couldn't remember which service station it was.

He looked sympathetic as he listened to her. 'Can you describe it?' he asked.

'It had a carpark, a restaurant and toilets,' she answered, with a smile, 'just like every other service station in the country.'

'Was it the first services that you came to?'

'Yes.'

'Can you remember which turning you took after the slip road?'

'I was following a lorry and it went right around the roundabout, almost full circle.' She was bemused by his questioning.

'That's junction 4a. I can take you there after work. Or if we both have a free lesson, we could go sooner.'

Judy was amazed and delighted. If she had known Reuben more, she would have hugged him. It hadn't occurred to her that the service station could be identified in that way. They arranged to meet at lunchtime to avoid the rush hour and Reuben was ready and waiting when Judy exited the college at twelve.

During the drive to the service station Reuben brought up the subject of Judy and Christine's falling out, once again. He asked her why they stilled lived together when they didn't get on.

'Well, we've only just moved into this house together and I haven't got the energy to find somewhere else yet, even though it is just about the worst place I have ever lived in. In fact, that's the only thing we both agree on.'

'So how come you moved in there in the first place if it is so bad?'

'It didn't seem so bad when we took it. There were other tenants, and it was so cheap, and we were desperate. Now it's just the two of us, it seems cold and creepy, as though it's a different house.'

'What about the landlord? Does he live nearby?' Reuben asked, with genuine interest.

'That's another strange thing. We've never met him. There was a card in a shop window. We phoned the number and a man told us the address. He said the other tenants would sort everything out. When we arrived, there was just a young couple there and we could choose our own rooms amongst the empty ones. We didn't even have to pay a deposit and couldn't believe our luck. But the couple moved out soon after and that's when we started noticing things.'

Reuben looked surprised. 'What things?' he asked curiously.

'Well, it's mostly a chilly feeling, particularly in certain rooms, but sometimes there are strange noises during the night too.' Judy realized how trivial it all sounded now she was telling Reuben and began to feel cross with herself for overreacting.

But Reuben was sympathetic. 'We don't know a house's history when it has been around for so many years. Maybe somebody died there, and their spirit hasn't found its way out of the house yet,' he suggested.

Judy was a little embarrassed as she hadn't imagined having this sort of conversation with a colleague that she hardly knew. Yet he was easy to talk to and she appreciated the way he didn't seem to make judgements about her. She toyed with the idea of inviting him over to see if he could feel anything unusual, but would he think she was coming on to him? The previous night had given her enough emotional turmoil to last a year, so she remained silent.

Meanwhile, Reuben had been thinking to himself, then said, 'I seem to remember reading something about those houses in the local paper a few years back. As far as I recall, the owners were offered money by property developers who wanted to build flats. I'm surprised the houses are still standing because they are pretty decrepit,'

'That must be why they are mostly empty,' said Judy. 'I wonder why the owner keeps it going. He can't make much money from the piddly rent he gets from us.'

'So, who have you been paying the rent to since that couple's gone?' he asked.

'They haven't moved far away so the boyfriend comes back to collect the rent once a week. He's still got a key, so we leave the money out for him.'

'That's very trusting of you,' he said. 'What if he just took it and made out that it had been stolen?'

'It's really not that much so I shouldn't think it would be worth the bother,' Judy said confidently. 'Besides, he doesn't seem to be capable of such deviousness; he's usually stoned.'

'Well, if you want, I could pop round sometime to see if I can feel anything weird. I'm not a ghostbuster or anything like that but people have told me I have a sixth sense.'

Judy took Reuben's last remark as a joke so laughed accordingly. 'If you have a spare hour, you are welcome to call around for a coffee,' she said, relieved that she hadn't been the one to suggest it.

An hour and fifty pounds later Judy arrived back at work and raised her thumb to Reuben as she went into her lesson. Soon she would be able to put the last twenty-four hours behind her and return to her normal life. It may be uneventful and boring, she thought, but that was how she liked it. The only thing she had left to do was face Christine who would be seething after her split from Gary. She would have to be careful not to slip up and say he was at the house. As soon as she got home, she would need to check the house for any traces of last night.

An unfamiliar car was parked in Judy's usual space when she arrived home; at least it was unfamiliar until the driver stepped out of it.

'Oh hi.'

'Hello, Judy. I'm sorry about earlier but I was in the middle of dealing with a client. I was genuine about driving you back to your car. You clearly managed alright without me though.'

'That's okay, Geoff. I was only phoning you for the name of the junction.'

'Yes. And how did you find out?'

'A colleague managed to work it out somehow then he took me in his car.'

'I'm glad everything turned out alright for you. And your friend? Have you made up?'

'Friend? Oh, you mean Christine. No. We haven't seen each other yet. She didn't turn up at work this morning so she's probably inside now.'

'Well. I wish you luck. See you around.' And then he got back inside his car and drove away.

Judy wondered whether Geoff wanted her to ask him in. Was she still indebted to him for last night's lift? Had she made it obvious that she didn't want him in the house? Well, why should she have asked him in? He was obviously lying about dealing with a client. She was an idiot, but not that much of an idiot.

Not long after Judy had gone inside, Christine also came home, uncharacteristically dishevelled, and hungover. Her head hurt and she felt sick. She had spent a large part of the morning sleeping, unable to remember much about the night before. When she saw Judy, she remembered how the evening had begun.

'Where were you last night? We went to the pub, and I left a note for you, but you didn't show up, so we went to Emma's party. You were invited too.'

Despite her questioning Christine no longer cared about Judy's excuses for not joining her and her ex-boyfriend in the pub. That was until she turned on the tap for some desperately needed cold water. Seeing the empty bottle of wine and two cups that were still in the sink she was curious, too curious to let it go. 'Have you been celebrating with someone?'

'Er, not really. More commiserating,' Judy replied. 'My car was broken into yesterday. They took my radio and I had to leave the car at the service station because my glasses were smashed. I needed something stronger than tea or coffee to relax after that.'

'How did you get home then?' Christine asked, while picking up each cup in turn.

'A man offered me a lift,' Judy explained, truthfully at first but noticing Christine was sniffing both cups, she added, 'I asked him in for a drink to thank him. It was going to be coffee, but he had some wine too, only a small one, of course, because he was driving?'

Christine looked amazed. 'You seem surprisingly spritely for someone who has just drunk almost a whole bottle of wine. It would take me more than half a day to recover from that. Judy, is there anything more you have to tell me about what happened here last night?'

Smiling, Judy winked playfully at Christine. Suddenly there was an awkward atmosphere as though neither woman wanted to be the next one to speak. Finally, Christine said she was going for a shower and then a lie-down. For her part, Judy wasn't sure how she felt about Christine anymore; scared, victorious, guilty. Maybe she was glad that they seemed to have put their quarrel behind them, and she was not going to spoil things by confessing to the previous night's sin.

Glasgow, September 1940

Dear Bertha,

Hoping you are well at this worrying time. I am so anxious about you being all alone in that old house and wish it were easier to visit. It is difficult to believe the way this war has turned into such violence and destruction, and of course heartache for you. Those terrible bombings that are happening in London must be terrifying for you and living so near the Docks, being as it is a major target. Perhaps it would be safer if you stayed with your husband's cousins until the bombings stop. Are you in contact with any of them? If not, I'm sure Edward would want you to be safer so he should ask them on your behalf.

We have also had bombs dropped on Glasgow though thankfully they have not been near our house. Many of the construction sites have closed due to the risk and for now, there is no work for James, even if he were fit. I wonder if he should join the Home Guard to take his mind off his own situation.

I think of the old days often and would give a lot to be back near you again, but James refuses to leave Glasgow. He says that it is years ahead of East London and people here are more outward-looking and ambitious. There will certainly be a need for reconstruction when this damned war is over. Surely it cannot last much longer. At times I care little about which side is victorious so long as it finishes soon.

James is desperate to be fit again as he feels so useless when he is unable to work. He does spend a lot of time in the library reading endless encyclopaedias about heating and plumbing. He is determined to build us our own house before he retires, though I have little confidence he will achieve that goal as you cannot build a house with words on pages. I can't see us ever leaving our tiny apartment but there's always room for you.

Look forward to hearing from you.

Yours with love,

Eveline

Chapter Fourteen

Christine wished that the water could wash away the memories of the previous night. It had been a miserable evening and she wished she had got that taxi home before the punch went to her head and anything seemed acceptable. How wrong she'd been about that Tristen and how on earth had things ended up as they had? At least there was no sign of him when she finally woke up. She wondered what Emma thought about what she had done, particularly as she had gone to the party with Gary. It would certainly be embarrassing the next time she went around to the house, that's if there was going to be a next time.

'Christine.'

The sound of her name disturbed her train of thought. She wasn't even sure how long she had been in the shower. Quickly wrapping her hair in a towel, she rushed down the stairs and into the kitchen, looking straight at Judy. 'What did you want?'

Judy glanced up briefly from her newspaper then returned to the local ads page. 'What do you mean?'

'Judy, why did you call me?'

'I didn't call you.'

'Yes, you did. I could hear you calling me while I was in the shower. I haven't had a chance to dry myself properly because I assumed it was urgent and now my dressing gown is soaking wet. And I didn't get a chance to put any conditioner on my hair.'

'Christine,' Judy said sternly, 'I did not call you. I haven't left the kitchen since you went upstairs. Why would I lie about that?'

The other woman's expression changed from annoyance to one of confusion as she had clearly heard the voice calling her name several times, cutting through the steam-filled bathroom and into the shower cubicle. There was no doubt about it. Of course, she assumed it was Judy calling her as who else could it be? There was nobody else in the house.

Judy could see the confused look on Christine's face and said, 'I've told you before I think this house is haunted. It's not just the horrible atmosphere. I hear things at night when no one else is here. There have been times when I've been so terrified, I can't move. It's ever since Russell and Tess moved out. And you said yourself that the kettle boiled on its own. I haven't had a chance to tell you, but I asked about it at work and everyone said a kettle couldn't switch itself on. It was not possible.'

'That's it. I can't live here anymore,' Christie cried. 'As soon as I come back after Christmas I'm moving out.'

'Do what you want,' Judy hit back, 'but you won't find me here when you get back. I am going to look for somewhere myself over the holidays and as soon as I find another place, I'll be gone. So good luck with your search.'

Silence fell for a few moments while both women considered their next move. There was no doubt that Judy had the upper hand in this confrontation. Christine would be away for three weeks from the following day, therefore, had no time to do anything until she returned. The last thing she wanted was to be returning to an empty house. For the first time she regretted not including Judy in her plans and began to back track.

'Oh, well, if you look for us while I'm away, I can leave you my deposit in case you find somewhere. You can have the best room for looking. I'll pack up my things ready so all you'll have to do is take them to our new place. We've never really liked this house, have we?'

So, now it was 'us', 'our' and 'we', Judy thought to herself smugly. No more singular pronouns. 'Okay. I'll start looking once the term is over. But I may have to sign a six-month contract, so you have to promise to keep your word and take up the other room.'

'Where else would I go Judy?'

The discussion ended abruptly at the sound of the doorbell ringing. They hadn't even known it worked as no one had ever rung it, probably because it was covered in cobwebs.

'Who on earth could that be?'

Christine's question struck Judy as a bit odd as the obvious person was Gary. Then she came back into the room, face white, followed by two police officers. One of them turned towards Christine before he began to speak.

'So, you are Christine Soyer? I'm afraid I have some bad news about your boyfriend, Gary Evans.'

'Have you arrested him?' Christine asked the question before he had a chance to finish what he was going to say.

'No. He was the victim of a serious assault early this morning and we need to ask you what you know about his movements leading up to the incident.'

Now Judy gasped and put her hand across her mouth to stop herself from saying anything. She was shocked to see Christine standing still, showing no emotion, then saying calmly, 'Is he dead?'

The police officers glanced at each other, also surprised at Christine's cold response to the news about her boyfriend. 'He is in a serious condition in hospital, and we are not able to speak to him yet so we are asking people who know him well for information that may help us catch the perpetrator.'

'He is not my boyfriend anymore. I dated him a few times but when I found out that he carried a knife, I finished with him. I didn't know he was that kind of person when I met him as I have never done anything bad in my entire life.'

'When did you last see him?' the second policeman asked her.

Water dripping down her forehead, Christine still managed to appear calm when she replied, 'Last night.'

'So, you were with him last night? I take it you were still his girlfriend at that point.' The police officer appeared annoyed at Christine's apparent unhelpfulness.

'We went to a party together, but he didn't stay long because I told him to leave. I found out about the knife as soon as we arrived and that's when I finished with him. He must have left about half-past ten and I didn't see him after that.'

'So, did he say why he carried a knife? Did you ever see him use it?' asked the other policeman.

'Good grief! No, I did not. I've already told you; I found the knife in his pocket when we got to the party, and I confronted him about it straight away. He told me he only carried it for self-defence, but I didn't believe him. He's a big enough man so he should be able to take care of himself without carrying an illegal weapon. It was clear that he was up to no good as you say.'

The second policeman was making notes in a little book while glancing at Judy. 'And you are …?'

She stammered while giving her name knowing that the attention was now on her.

'When did you see him last?' he asked without taking his eyes off her.

Judy knew her face and neck were crimson and probably screaming like a siren, but she found herself lying, nevertheless. 'It was yesterday afternoon, you know, Christine, when I gave him a lift here. I went out not long after and he and Christine had gone by the time I got home.' Was she perverting the course of justice by not telling them about what had really happened late last night? Yet how could she confess to sleeping with Gary with Christine standing right opposite her?

Christine's eyes left Judy and returned to the police officer. 'Yes, that's correct. I hadn't known about the knife then.'

It was clear from the tone of the police officers that they assumed Gary's assault was drug-related, therefore, they didn't waste any more time with the two women.

'We'll see ourselves out,' one said, after handing Christine a leaflet which immediately dropped out of her hand.

'Are you alright, Christine?'

'Of course. Why do you ask?'

'But you must feel something, even if he did carry a knife. Perhaps he was telling the truth. It was only a small knife.'

Christine stared at Judy who immediately regretted her words.

'How do you know how big it was?'

'I didn't. I just guessed it must be small if it was in his pocket. You don't think he's violent, do you?'

'I don't care what he is, but I'm wondering why you do.'

Judy shrugged her shoulders and left the room, the conversation becoming more and more uncomfortable. Christine glanced down at the leaflet lying on the floor and slowly picked it up. It offered support for families of assault victims. For the first time her eyes welled with tears. If she had not finished with him at the party, Gary would not have been stabbed and she would not have stayed all night at the party drunk glasses of punch, smoked something rotten, and worse of all be ashamed of her one-night stand with the man she had been convinced was gay. But it was too late now. She screwed the leaflet into a ball and dropped it into the bin.

Judy lay on her bed in the foetal position unable to comprehend all the events of the last few hours. She could still smell Gary on her pillow and soon he could be dead. How much longer would this rollercoaster last? From what the police said it sounded as though Gary had been stabbed on his way home after leaving her, as though it were some sort of punishment. Perhaps Christine was right, and she should always be by herself. That way she would not ruin other people's lives.

Glasgow, October 1940

James's eyes were fixated on the dying embers of the fire, the final pieces of coal glowing bravely before they faded to darkness. Eveline watched him as though he were an actor in a film. James Cagney or Clark Gable. But this was their lives not some dreary movie. She knew that her husband was unhappy but there was little she could do to help him. When they first moved to Scotland they had been young and filled with the hope and optimism that love brings. That initial magic had long ceased to cover the misery of everyday life when there was no money for small pleasures. They remained in the same place with the same work, yet older and more cynical.

'A penny for your thoughts,' she said, trying to sound cheerful and unaware of his mood. However, it was as if he had not heard her words or chose to ignore them. Her attention returned to the half-made jumper she was knitting and immediately she noticed a dropped stitch. Suddenly he turned his head towards her, his eyes only half focussed on her.

'I think we should take in a lodger,' he said slowly. 'There's a man I use to work with who knows people looking for a room. We could do with the extra money, and we have a room sitting empty.'

Eveline winced at the mention of the empty room. Empty of children is what her husband meant. Had he now given up on the idea of a family? Perhaps she should have told him the truth before they married but it didn't seem fair that she had to sacrifice everything for something that wasn't her fault. No. She was content with James. Although the tenement apartment they lived in was small and dark, it was their home, and it gave her some small comfort in her grim life. It was like a sanctuary from the world outside which had failed her. And she no longer wanted a part of that world.

But James was different. He needed company and her company alone was not enough. He had been happiest in the mornings when he was leaving for work, on his way to building and banter with his workmates. But the war had taken many men of James's age away and left him as one of the few who had not gone. Work was no longer the cheerful place for James that it had been, rather a place of shame.

'Maybe for a few months,' she agreed. 'See how things are then. Or maybe until this war is over. I'd prefer a female lodger if possible. I don't want to dry my clothes in front of a strange man.'

James nodded then returned to his thoughts.

Chapter Fifteen

It was Christine's last night in the house before going back to France for the Christmas break. But it was not a restful one. It began about three o'clock. A clanking sound reverberated around the house. Was it inside or outside? It wasn't clear. Upstairs a terrified Christine was listening at her bedroom door to a thumping sound on the landing. She was desperate to get downstairs without having to open her door, but her window was too high from the ground.

Meanwhile on the ground level, Judy was convinced it was outside in the yard and was afraid that it might come through her window. She made the decision to spend the night upstairs in one of the spare rooms, which would surely be safer than hers. However, just as she was about to get up, the location of the sound seemed to shift to inside the house, more precisely in the hallway. It sounded like a bicycle chain rotating. Was someone riding a bicycle inside the house? But that would be absurd and there was no bicycle in the house to ride. Suddenly it was outside her room, getting louder and louder until it stopped. She heard a tapping at her door, and she tried to scream but nothing would come out of her trembling mouth. The door handle turned slowly, and she thought she would die of fright. Then, to her relief, she heard Christine's trembling voice whispering her name.

'Christine, what was that noise? Was it you?'

'I thought it was you. It seemed to be coming from down here so how could it be me? I was terrified but couldn't stay up there on my own. What on earth could it be Judy? It sounded like chains moving.'

'Yes,' Judy agreed, 'or something made of metal. At first it seemed to be coming from outside my window, then it moved into the hall. That's when I thought that I would surely die.'

'That's crazy,' Christine said, still whispering, as though she was afraid that she might be heard. 'I thought it was coming from the backyard too until it all went quiet outside. Then it started up again but inside the house. Do you think someone has broken in? Maybe we should call the police even though I have had enough of them to last a lifetime.'

Christine was almost in tears which Judy thought was not helping the situation as they needed to think clearly. They stared at each other, both afraid to speak. The clanking noise had stopped and there was an eerie silence which was almost as bad. Suddenly they heard a different sound, that of someone, or something, running down the stairs. Christine screamed and slammed Judy's bedroom door shut from inside.

No sooner had the footsteps begun, they stopped. There was no sound of the front door opening or footsteps moving through the passageway into the kitchen. Was somebody standing outside the door, just a few feet away from them? By now Judy was out of her bed and holding a pair of scissors that she had taken from her work bag. They were not large but had to be better than nothing.

'Judy, what are you going to do?' Christine was struggling to sound coherent due to her trembling mouth.

Judy was strangely calm. 'I don't think there is anyone out there. Not anymore anyway.'

She walked past Christine and opened her bedroom door to find her hunch was correct. The hallway was empty, so Judy proceeded towards the bedroom next to hers.

By now Christine was standing directly behind her, determined not to be left on her own. 'Do you think he could be in there? I didn't hear the door go.'

They both held their breath as Judy opened the door and switched on the light. She walked over to the wardrobes and opened the doors of each one while wondering what she would do if someone or something was hiding inside. There was nothing. That room too was empty apart from the furniture and old piano. After that there was only the sitting room and the kitchen left and neither room showed any signs of an intruder having been there.

'It must have been squatters next door,' Judy said. She wasn't sure who she was trying to convince.

'But it sounded much nearer,' Christine argued. 'Can I sleep in here with you? I'm too scared to go back upstairs. He might have crept back up there.'

Judy was silently relieved that Christine had jumped in first with what she herself had been about to suggest. All the same she acted as though it was an imposition. 'Okay but you'll have to drag one of those mattresses in here. You're not sharing my bed.'

Christine left the following morning after propping the spare mattress back up against the banister where it had been when they first moved in. She appeared amused at the thought of leaving Judy alone in the house for three weeks. Given the terror of what they had just both experienced, Christine's lack of sensitivity angered her housemate so much Judy had fleetingly considered confessing about her fling with Gary. Nevertheless, having belatedly found Christine's note about going to the pub the night before, she held her tongue. If Gary had mentioned it, the night may have ended up differently. But it was too late for regrets now.

It had been an exhausting week and she still had one more day of work until she finished for the Christmas holidays. Although struggling to keep her eyes open, she decided to get away from the house for the day and clear her mind. Spending a few hours at the museums would help her to put any worries out of her mind, at least until later.

At the National Portrait Gallery Richard III's eyes stared into a long-forgotten distance. The frame that held his portrait seemed ridiculously small for such a giant of history. Nostalgia surged through Judy's heart. Her time as a student had been the happiest in her life. Immersed in the medieval world of kings, wars, and deception, she had greedily gobbled up the words of every relevant book in the dusty Swansea University library. She loved defending the much-maligned Richard in her essays. she cried when Henry II learnt of his son's betrayal while on his deathbed. She was entranced by poor Queen Isabella's tragic romance with Roger Mortimer. For three wonderful years she was engrossed in the turmoil and tragedy of the lives of other people, people who had died centuries and centuries ago. It had been hard to leave their world and re-enter her own.

Her thoughts were broken by a loudspeaker advising visitors that the gallery was about to close, and she made her way out into the cold London street. Charring Cross station was its usual chaotic self so, as it was a dry evening, she decided to walk home along the river. The Thames Embankment was bustling with tourists, and she enjoyed the gasps of awe and wonder that filled the air. It was a welcome change from the soulless experience of a tube journey.

Outside one of the entrances to Victoria Embankment Gardens a talented street artist was entertaining a crowd of spectators and people passing turned their heads to see what the fuss was about. One man, however, wasn't interested in the spectacle. Although standing with the crowd, he was looking one way and another, as though waiting for someone. A pickpocket, perhaps, waiting to ruin the enjoyment of someone's day. Judy pulled her jacket closer and walked on.

Half an hour passed and, with the walk becoming more and more deserted, she opted to catch a bus for the final stretch of her journey home. She sat behind a young woman nestling a baby in one hand while trying to confine a bored toddler to his seat with the other. Judy preferred buses to trains and tubes. They were a welcome reminder that there was an existence to London beyond tourists and commuters – her London.

The bus jolted to a stop to allow an out-of-breath passenger to board. It was the man who had been watching the crowd – the 'pickpocket'. She looked over her shoulder to see him sitting one row behind on the opposite side of the aisle. He was watching her. Had he followed her onto the bus? Her mind went into overdrive. She couldn't let him follow her back to her house. It was three stops away. The young woman in front of her rang the bell and stood up ready to get off the bus. Somehow it made Judy panic more. As the woman strapped her baby into its pushchair, the bus stopped to allow her to exit. Judy braced herself. The doors opened then just as they were about to close, she rushed down the aisle and squeezed through. The bus moved on as the man watched through the window. He was standing near the door.

The evening arrived too soon and at half-past six Judy was back at the house, facing the first night of three weeks alone. After the frightening experience of her journey home, Judy had thought about sleeping in Christine's room that night. She eventually decided against it since she would be 'trapped' at the end of the house, unable to get out. At least in her own room, she had a window that she could get out of, and she would be able to hear if someone were moving out in the hallway. After twenty minutes of mental escape routes, she reprimanded herself; it was going to be a long three weeks with that attitude. She had spent many nights alone in a house before this without worrying about ghosts and intruders. Therefore, she would make herself some supper, watch television and go to bed when she was tired. The same as everyone else.

An hour later she was curled up on the settee watching Friends, which, to her surprise, she enjoyed immensely. The only thing that annoyed her was that it was about flatmates who all got on brilliantly. She knew it was fiction and no young people had such amazing apartments even if they had great mates. Friends was followed by a film starring Sharon Stone. Another fabulous apartment but, as it featured a serial killer, Judy wasn't quite so envious. Give me ghosts over serial killers any day, she thought. Nevertheless, that night she slept on the settee with both the light and the television on.

Glasgow, October 1940

Two days later Dot moved into the small bedroom in the tenement apartment. She managed to pick up a single bed and wardrobe from the Salvation Army store, reducing the cost of preparing the room. Dot was a cheerful woman who worked in one of the temporary kitchens erected to serve the workmen building the many corporation houses on the outskirts of the city. With her light blonde hair and blue eyes, she looked more Scandinavian than British. The musical inflections in her accent suggested her origins may have been in the northeast islands of Scotland, as did her companionable personality and hardiness. Eveline wondered about her background but did not like to ask. It was none of her business. She understood why some people preferred to keep their past to themselves -or even forget they had a past.

Dot settled in quickly and made herself useful in ways that a male lodger would not have. The removal of so many able-bodied people had brought all sorts of mavericks to the surface. Dot was likely one of those. On her day off she would go to the public washhouse rather than use Eveline's washboard and bucket, happily taking some of the couple's larger items to do. Because she worked the later shifts, she often brought home leftover food from the work's kitchen, which she shared with Eveline and James. For all her favours, Dot never asked for anything in return, not a reduction in rent nor any extra comforts. Eveline had no reason to dislike her. Nonetheless, she did, and she felt bad for it, which made her dislike Dot even more.

Chapter Sixteen

Judy decided that it had not been such a wise decision to sleep on an old and broken settee. That night she would go back to the bed with two mattresses. A knock on the front door caused her to forget her aches and she hurriedly brushed herself down before rushing to open it. A young man stood outside smiling.

'Hi,' he said. 'I heard there is a room to rent. Can I look around?'

A surprised Judy let him in, apologising for not being aware that he was coming and for the untidy state of the sitting room. He was the first person to view the house since she and Christine had a few months earlier and they had given up on the hope that someone else would move in. Her first impression of the man was that he was rather rough-looking, but she had also thought that about Gary.

'I'm Judy,' she said, smiling, determined not to be the unfriendly woman Christine had accused her of being. 'Would you like a tea or coffee? I'm just about to make one.'

'Yeah, okay. Either would be good. Milk and two sugars. My name's Steve by the way. I'll go on and take a quick peep while you are making it.'

'The first room on the right is mine and the room next to the bathroom is taken but all the others are vacant,' she called after him as he ran up the stairs, wondering what he would make of the attic room. Was he willing to sleep on a rolled-up piece of foam like Badger?

While she was waiting for the kettle to boil she wondered what she should say if he wanted a room. Was it up to her to say yes? If only Russell had left a telephone number or an address. Then she remembered that they had rung the landlord from a phone box so Steve must have rung him from there too. She supposed it must be okay then. She could hear him opening and closing doors, moving beds around, opening windows. He was certainly having a good look around.

He finally came down the stairs and she heard him go into her room. She shouted out that it was the front room which was vacant, and he reappeared apologetically. Back in the kitchen he sat down with his tea and asked Judy about the other tenant. She explained that Christine was away but did not tell him for how long. He told her he was surprised to find so many empty rooms.

'It's a big old house for two people,' he said. 'How do the bills work out? I bet they are expensive.'

'No, not really,' she told him. 'We only have to pay a proportion of the bills as if the house were full. It's generous of the landlord as he must be subsidising us. If you move in, the bills will go down even more.'

'So, it's just the room next to yours and the two front rooms upstairs that are free, is it?' he asked her.

'And the top room. Didn't you see it? The door can be difficult to notice when you are in a hurry. If you want, I will take you back up and show you.' She was already walking towards the stairs.

'Sounds good,' he agreed, as he got to his feet. Then, he changed his mind. 'I'm going to look at one in another place in town before I decide so I'll come back soon if I want a room here. Thanks for the tea.' And as abruptly as he had entered the house, he left.

Judy was surprised that he didn't immediately take a room as he wouldn't find one half as cheap anywhere else in the area. He had seemed a lot happier leaving the house than when he arrived, so she had assumed he was pleased with what he had seen. Cringing at the thought of him being in her room she hoped that there were no dirty clothes on the floor and looked in to check.

Her room was tidy, her bed was made, and the floor was clear. She went through all the rooms wondering which one would have looked the most impressive to Steve or had he been put off by something. Christine's room was the only one that didn't look old and shabby; the others could easily have been in a different house.

On opening the front bedroom door, she noticed that the top of the piano was open. Someone had lifted it up since the last time she had been in the room. Then she felt a slight draught. There was a freshness in the air that was unfamiliar, and she walked over to the window to investigate. Yes, a window was open, not wide but an inch from the top. The catch of the sash was unlocked, and the window had slumped down, allowing the outside air into the stale, dusty room. How had it come undone? She had made sure all the windows were locked before Christine left, or had she missed that one? Did Steve go into that room? She thought he hadn't, but maybe, if he had, he opened the window to check if it was secure. Why? It could be innocent. Yes, it probably was innocent. Of course, he wanted to make sure the house he moved into was secure she thought as she locked the window once more. Looking at the old wooden sash frames she knew that it wasn't at all secure and she was glad that she had decided to start looking around for somewhere else to live. In fact, she would do that as soon as she finished work later.

As it was the end of term and the lessons were finished, the tiny college staffroom was filled with the sound of happy voices winding down for Christmas. Judy and Reuben sat together enjoying a mince pie with their coffee.

'Are you going home now?' he asked her.

'Yes. I've got an appointment with the local ads, more specifically, the rooms to rent page.'

'Well, I am free to come and look around. I can follow you in my car.'

'What, now?' She had already forgotten the conversation they had had about the house.

'It's ok if you have something else to do,' he responded quickly.

Judy was tired and not in the mood for entertaining. Then she scolded herself for showing her lack of enthusiasm after he had gone to so much trouble for her. 'No, Reuben, it's fine. Just give me five minutes head start to check the state of the place.'

It was more like twenty minutes after she got home that Reuben pulled up in his Morris 1000. There weren't many cars slower than hers, she thought watching him get out and lock the door.

'It's lonely around here,' he said, while looking up and down the street. 'I suppose it's quiet. No late-night parties at least.'

'I know. I think it's the part of London that people forgot,' she laughed. 'Anyway, welcome to our abode.'

She led Reuben through the house, starting with the characteristically warm attic.

'And you turned this room down because…?' he laughed.

Judy cringed when remembering her determination to see the attic room. What on earth would Reuben have made of her sleeping on a rolled-up piece of foam?

As they made their way through the rest of the house Judy tried to picture each room as Reuben probably did. The cracks in the walls were more numerous than she remembered. Finally, she took him out into the yard where he looked at the extension that housed the bathroom and Christine's bedroom, then walked over to the shed, at which point he stood almost as if in a trance. Once back inside he was silent for a minute before sharing his thoughts with Judy.

'There's definitely a hostile atmosphere in the front three rooms,' he commented 'but I also felt it to a lesser extent in the two middle bedrooms. The back rooms are fine, but the yard is hostile which doesn't really follow a pattern, otherwise the property would become more passive the further back it goes. What is in the shed?'

'I don't know as I've not been in it. I've just looked through the window. There's some old bike that's been left, but that's as much as I could see,' she said.

'And you said that Christine has felt something too.'

'Yes, but she doesn't spend as much time here as I do, and I doubt she's here much on her own. That's when you really notice things.'

'You shouldn't spend so much time by yourself.' He stared at her for a few seconds.

'I don't mind my own company. It's better than most people's,' she laughed.

'Is there anything in the house that's old, I mean, like an ornament or a mirror? Something that might have been here for a long time,' he asked.

'Yes. In here.' She walked into her bedroom. He followed her.

'I found this in the attic room the other day. I'm sure it wasn't there before.' She handed him the photograph of Eveline. 'Maybe it belonged to a previous owner. It says 1941 so they are probably both dead, I mean the owner and this Eveline woman. Unless they are one and the same person.'

'Not necessarily,' Reuben said, 'If this woman were, say, 40 in 1941, she would be in her nineties now and that's not unheard of, particularly in women. Do you think this could have anything to do with the unwelcoming presence in this house?'

Judy shuddered at his use of the word 'presence' as it gave a more physical element to what she had considered being just a feeling.

'Are you okay?' he said, handing back the photograph.

As Judy took it back, he held onto it just long enough to cause her to look up. There was something in the way he was gazing at her that made her feel uncomfortable, so she began to step back into her personal space. Suddenly he grabbed her wrist and was leaning in towards her as though intending to kiss her. She jumped up and clumsily collected the coffee cups, and, as if nothing had happened, thanked him for coming around.

He looked confused for a minute, but she thought he was pretending. 'What's the matter? I thought -'

'I've got a bit of a headache, Reuben. I think I'm going to have a lie down for a while. I'll see you soon.'

'But I thought that's what you wanted,' he said defensively. 'Why did you let me come here if you weren't interested?'

Now it was Judy who looked confused. With exasperation, she replied, 'You asked to come around, Reuben. You said it was to check the atmosphere of the house.'

'Judy, surely you know that a man only pays attention to a woman if he is attracted to her?' He stormed past her and left the house without saying goodbye.

Was Reuben's red face caused by embarrassment or anger? Judy didn't know and neither did she care, at least for the moment. It was a clumsy move at an inappropriate moment. He had behaved like an inexperienced teenager and had caused her as much embarrassment as himself. On the other hand, had she been leading him on, she wondered? She certainly hadn't known that about men, but it made sense when she remembered Gary's sudden interest in her the night before. It also made her wonder about the man at the service station and what his intentions were.

Glasgow, December 1940

It was late evening on a cold wet Sunday, and Eveline, James, and their lodger, Dot were sitting around a wooden table playing cards. There was no money involved, of course, so they used Ludo pieces instead. Dot was winning, probably because she was trying harder than everyone else. It seemed wrong to Eveline that they should be playing cards on a Sunday but the other two had laughed and told her it was a bigger sin to drop bombs on people's homes.

Although James hadn't been able to work much since the war had got so terrible, they were able to manage with the money that Bertha sent them every month. Eveline thought that James would be too proud to accept charity, however, after making a few hollow comments, he agreed that they would struggle to keep going without it, even with Dot's rent. When his foot was better they hoped he would be able to get some work at the builders' yard. He had been much more cheerful since Dot moved in, probably as it was someone else to talk to. And Dot was always laughing and joking, in contrast to his wife.

As for Eveline, the last few years had seen her become a shadow of her former self, going through the motion of a dull life with no interest in anything. She never left the tenement except to take out the rubbish and go to the shop for groceries. Her dull existence hadn't bothered her too much before but lately, since they had been back in contact, she was comparing herself negatively to her younger sister. Eveline had gone to Haworth intending to earn a living and better herself but now she felt as dependent on charity as she had been at the orphanage. In contrast, Bertha had stayed longer, become educated, and married well. She would never want for anything.

Perhaps leaving at such a young age had been the wrong decision. However, Eveline knew that she could never have stayed on at the orphanage, not after what had happened.

Chapter Seventeen

A spurt of cold water hit Judy's naked back and she pressed herself, as much as she could, against the plastic door of the shower cubicle in an impossible attempt to miss the icy blast. Come on! come on! Please warm-up. And slowly, but surely, the cold trickle heated to a tepid, bearable temperature. Judy dived under the pitiful spray in a desperate attempt to wet herself as quickly as she could in case the cold water made an unwelcome comeback.

A few minutes passed before enough water came through the shower head to sufficiently wet her long thick hair and she quickly rubbed some shampoo into a thick lather and worked it into her damp curls. As the warm suds flowed down her face Judy relaxed and enjoyed the moment. The bathroom, unlike much of the rest of the house, was bright and clean with a pleasant atmosphere. It could be a bathroom in any modern house with its white walls and fitted suite.

Steam was now settling on the shower cubicle walls and she snapped out of her dreamlike state as she noticed it. Had she forgotten to put the extractor fan on? Better get a move on she thought to herself, rinsing the great accumulation of lather out of her hair while trying to rub soap over her body. The saying less haste, more speed came into her mind as she dropped the soap. She crouched down and felt blindly for the soap bar as the cubicle was now filled with steam.

Suddenly, behind one of the steamed-up walls, a shadow moved. Judy's heart was racing at a pace that seemed impossible. What was that? There was no one else in the house. Or was there? Had she locked the front door, made sure the windows were closed? Probably not. That's what comes of being less afraid of what's outside than inside the house. She found herself whimpering as she stared at the cubicle door, expecting it to open at any second. The steam continued to fill the cubicle and was now filling up the whole of the bathroom. It was impossible to see anything, even the walls of the cubicle that were only inches from her.

Slowly Judy stood up, turned off the shower, and started to rub some of the steam off the cubicle door. She pulled the towel down and wrapped it around her still soapy body. The shower had now decreased to a single drip which allowed Judy to hear the whirring of the extractor fan. So she had switched it on.

She pushed open the cubicle door bracing herself for whatever lay waiting behind it. She peered out before stepping onto the bathroom floor and holding her arms out. Already the steam had begun to disperse, and she opened the small bathroom window to help it on its way. She could see that the bathroom was empty, besides her, and the bathroom door was closed as it had been before. Tentatively she pulled open the bathroom door.

A slight chill greeted her as she stepped out onto the landing, and she was hit with the realization of what could have happened. She peered over the banister to see the source of the colder air – the front door was open. Dressed only in the towel she jumped into Christine's bedroom and closed the door. Shivering she was horrified at how vulnerable she was at that moment; alone, naked with no escape. She rummaged through Christine's wardrobe looking for something to cover herself with. Wearing a mini dress, she slowly opened the door and shouted out,

'Is there anybody there? Reuben!'

Judy didn't know what she would do if Reuben appeared in front of her.

Nothing. What should she do? Then she heard footsteps. Where were they coming from? They were getting louder and louder, heavier, and heavier. They had turned into thudding sounds on the stairs but were they getting closer or further away, she could not tell. She slammed the bedroom door shut once again and ran to the window. The drop onto the hard concrete was far too high. There was no way out, she was trapped. The sound of the footsteps seemed to be coming from several different directions and she wondered how many other people were in the house. Then a door slamming. It had to be the front door making that much noise.

Once again she opened the bedroom door and crept out onto the landing. She was expecting to see the other bedroom doors open, but they were closed, although the single panel door leading to the attic was open. They must have been up there, she decided, and she began to descend the staircase. The front door was now closed, and Judy knew that whoever had been in the house a few moments ago was gone.

Half an hour later Judy was sitting in the lounge, sipping a hot cup of tea, and wondering what exactly had just happened. Did the front door open itself? Was she naked in the shower while an intruder was in the house? Remembering the shadow in the bathroom, she shuddered. Was he in there with her? Maybe she should report this to the police. Yes, that's what she'd do. She picked up the Yellow Pages and began to leaf through it for the nearest police station while rehearsing the impending conversation.

I want to report an intruder in my house.
Was it a male or a female?
I don't know. I didn't see them clearly. I am sure it was a man though.
OK. Where was he?
In the bathroom.
Did you see him in the bathroom?
Yes, well, I saw a shadow.

136

Just a shadow? You didn't actually see his face or body?

No, but…

Did he say anything?

I don't think so. Well, you see, I was in the shower.

And you saw his shadow through the shower curtains. Was he wearing a wig and a dress by any chance?

Judy put down the Yellow Pages. Maybe it wasn't a shadow after all, but her eyes playing tricks on her. Perhaps the shampoo had got into her eyes and affected her vision. Or maybe it *was* a shadow, but one of a bird flying outside the window, rather than a human inside the bathroom. Yes, that's what it was. Probably. But she didn't imagine the footsteps and the door slamming. There must have been someone in the house, but it was probably a burglar who was used to opening old front doors. When he realized the house was filled with nothing costing more than a few quid he left.

Then she remembered the gold bracelet that she had bought for her birthday and a sinking feeling swept through her. Any burglar worth his salt would have grabbed that, she thought to herself, as she made her way towards her bedroom. But the bangle was still by the side of her bed where she had left it. So it hadn't been a burglar after all. Rather it was someone who knew exactly what he was looking for. Something upstairs in the attic.

Later as the light was beginning to fade, Judy remembered about the bathroom window. Although the window was small, she was not taking any chances. She climbed the stairs intending to shut it, noticing as she did a piece of soiled paper wrapped around one of the balustrades. Yuck! She went to the bathroom and pulled off a piece of toilet paper to pick it up with. It must have blown in through the window. Looking more closely, however, she saw that the soil was in fact handwriting – someone's address: 12 Market Road. This address!

It was an envelope but an old one, which had yellowed with age. She held it in her hands now, discarding the toilet paper, and squinted at the name at the top of the address. Unable to make it out she opened the envelope and took out the letter inside.

Dear Bertha,

I felt the need to write this letter having spent much time thinking about the past twenty years. While tidying my cabinet, I found a locket that our mother had given to me before she died. The photographs inside were taken of us at the Coronation street party though I doubt you will remember that as you were just a little one. While she was on her death bed, she made me promise that I would look after you, my little sister, and always be there for you.

You will remember that I was deeply affected by what happened to me at the orphanage and needed to leave there as soon as I found employment. It is to my deep regret that I did not keep my promise and stay with you or wait until you were old enough to come with me. If I could turn the clocks back, I would do things differently, but I made my choices and must live with them, for better or worse.

Things have not been easy for either of us, but at least we have each other now. Having the locket kept a part of you with me over these last twenty years but I would like you to have it now we are reunited. Try to remember me as I am in the locket as this is how I will always remember you.

Yours with love,
Eveline

Judy felt a weird sensation running through her body. She was reading actual correspondence between two sisters from over fifty years ago. The letter was genuine, there was no doubt; the paper used, the beautiful cursive handwriting, the formality of language even between friends or family members. Would they still be alive, she wondered? Which coronation was she referring to? Judy knew every king and his reign until Henry VIII but by the time she got to the 20th century, she was reduced to Elizabeth II. And it clearly wasn't referring to the current monarch's coronation as the letter was dated 1941.

Then Judy gasped. The year of the letter was the same as the photograph and the writer was Eveline. Of course! The woman in the photograph was the same woman who had written this letter. But why had it suddenly appeared?

London, December 1940

Bertha did not mind sending money to Eveline as she had more than she needed. A wealthy widow, she would never have to worry where her next meal was coming from. Unlike Eveline. Yet something bothered her. It wasn't James' fault that he didn't receive compensation when he broke his foot; or that he was unable to work. But it was almost a year later. Somehow, she didn't believe there was no work available as she had seen signs for skilled workers, even outside the army recruitment office. So many men had gone abroad to fight, there was a shortage of electricians, plumbers, and carpenters. It was surely the same in such a big city as Glasgow.

Edward had inherited a fair sum from his parents, and he used it wisely. To give his wife security he immediately paid off their mortgage, and now the house belonged to Bertha. In the event of her death, it would go to Eveline, her next of kin. However, it bothered Bertha that Eveline was childless. What if Eveline should die before her husband - her out-of-work husband who had not even joined the Home Guard? For this reason, she visited her solicitor and made a change in her will.

Chapter Eighteen

The next day Russell called for the rent and Judy asked him what he knew about the landlord. He seemed a little bemused by her interest but told her what little he knew.

The owner of the house was a man called Stan who lived somewhere in Scotland. When Russell first moved in, there was another tenant who took the rent and paid the utility bills, but he left after a few months and offered Russell 'the job'. Basically, he lived rent-free if he acted as quasi landlord and looked after things so that Stan did not have to bother.

Judy was still sceptical about Russell's willingness to keep coming back to a property he no longer lived at, but she pushed it out of her mind.

'It's funny you should say he lives in Scotland,' she commented. 'It's just that I have come across a few things from Glasgow so this house must have been in his family for decades.'

'What things have you come across?' asked Russell, with an eyebrow raised. He was finally asking a question of his own as opposed to reluctantly answering them.

Judy proceeded to recount her discovery of the photograph in the attic and the letter on the staircase, omitting the experience she had had in the shower. She knew the young man was probably thinking she was crazy, but it didn't stop her. The thought of staying in the house for three weeks, with nothing but the strange atmosphere and noises to keep her company, was too much to bear.

The letter and photograph had provided her with a welcome distraction.

'I'm wondering if there are more letters and photographs in the attic. In fact, I might do a little exploring over the holidays to kill some time. I find it fascinating to think that other people were living in this house, standing where we are now so many years ago.'

The young man had a surprised expression on his face for a fleeting moment, before just as soon seeming to lose interest. Then he walked away. He didn't even turn around when he said, 'Whatever rocks your boat, I suppose. As long as you don't go hitting walls down.'

But Judy called him back. 'By the way, that guy who viewed the house and said he would be in touch, have you heard back from him?'

Russell pulled a confused expression. 'No idea what you are talking about. There's been no interest in the house since you moved in. You should be careful who you let in.'

That evening Judy put any irrational fears to the back of her mind and climbed both sets of stairs leading to the attic room. It was not something she could have imagined doing even twenty-four hours ago, but her curiosity had got the better of her. When she opened the door she noticed how warm the air inside felt and could see how someone might like it.

It was a pleasant little room and she wondered what Bertha had used it for all those years ago; a nursery perhaps, if there had been children. But she remembered that the letter had mentioned Bertha being alone in the house. Maybe her children had grown up, she thought. Or perhaps they were not yet born at the time of the letter. She had no idea how old Bertha was in 1941 but Eveline looked fortysomething. Although, the fashion for men and women at that time was ageing so she could even have been as young as thirty. Judy cringed at that thought. Was that how old she looked to other people. To Gary?

The little cupboard door was closed which cast doubt on her theory that the letter had somehow been blown out of it. Or maybe it was in the habit of opening and closing when it was windy. It would have been with the front door open. As she crouched down to open the tiny door, she remembered the icy draught that came out of it when they had first viewed the room. She hesitated for a few seconds before pulling the handle slowly. There was no draught this time.

The photograph lay where she had left it, but she could see nothing else. She put her right hand inside and patted the floor to see how big the space was, but she could not feel any walls that would confine any objects. It was not the compact space a typical cupboard offers. Slowly, she lay down on the carpet so that she could fully stretch out her left arm in the direction of the dark unknown space.

It was surprising how far back the cupboard stretched, and she realized she wouldn't be able to access it all. Suddenly her hand touched something soft, and she screamed, banging her head against the little door as she retracted her arm. What was that, she thought? Could it have been a spider? Judy was terrified of house spiders, but she told herself it was a visual phobia, and, as long as she could not see their long brown legs scurrying across the floor, it was fine.

Once again she put her arm back inside the space, inching it along the wooden floorboards inside. This time there was no soft obstruction. She didn't know whether to be relieved as that made it more likely that it had been a spider. Her hand finally encountered something hard and pushing her arm to the limit she managed to grip the object at the top and slide it towards the opening.

It was a decorative wooden box, the kind that people collect keepsakes in. Tiny blue flowers were carved near the edge of the lid – Forget Me Nots. It was closed with a metal clasp and when she shook it, she heard the light fluttering of paper inside and wondered if they were more letters. She stared at it for a while, feeling a pang of guilt that she was about to look through someone else's personal possessions, while at the same time excited at the thought of finding out more about Bertha and Eveline's lives. Picking up the solitary photograph of Eveline, she shut the little door and left the room just as the telephone began to ring.

'Judy, it's Christine. Have you found anywhere yet?'

'Give me a chance. I only just finished work yesterday.'

'But there are only a few days left until Christmas. What else have you got to do, Judy?'

'I'll start first thing in the morning. It'll only take a day. You know I enjoy house hunting.'

'I think you are being optimistic. Anyway, ring me back when you have got somewhere.'

The following morning was proving to be more disheartening than enjoyable. Each appointment had felt as though the other tenants were viewing her rather than the other way around.

'Where are you from?' 'What is your idea of a good night out?' 'There are a few more people to see.' 'We'll let you know in the following couple of days.'

However, she knew they wouldn't. By the time she left the third property, she felt utterly dejected. After buying a new Free Ads paper, she made her way back home.

While circling houses in cheaper areas, Judy already dreaded any further viewings. Perhaps if Christine were with her, they would have more success. It was always more difficult when you were on your own, she told herself. If only she hadn't fallen out with Reuben, she could have asked him to accompany her. Perhaps she still could. Other than Christine, he was the only person she knew. Or was he? What about that man at the service station, Geoff? He might know people who rented rooms. It was worth a shot.

'It's blue with Saxon College written on it,' Judy said down the phone, trying to forget she was a terrible liar at the best of times. 'I'm sure I took it with me before leaving and it wasn't in the car when I collected it from the service station.'

'I haven't noticed it, but it might have blown onto the back seat. If you hang on a minute, I'll check.' There was an uncomfortable pause and she wondered if he was going to end the call, but then his voice became warmer. 'How are you, anyway? I hope you have recovered from that nasty experience. You really should have let me take you to collect your car. I was waiting for you to ring.'

Judy reprimanded herself for thinking of Geoff as a creep. He sounded genuinely kind, and she wished that she had taken up his offer of a lift back to the service station. Then there would have been no embarrassing encounter with Reuben, who really was a creep.

'Yes, I have recovered Geoff and I want to thank you for helping me. It was so kind of you to offer but I was still in shock the next morning and just wanted to get things over and done with. Anyway, I want to thank you properly. What do you drink? I am going to buy you a bottle of something.'

'You can buy me a coffee then,' he said cheerily. 'I'll pick you up in an hour and that way we can look for your parking permit together.'

Judy paused before answering. Was he asking her on a date? Don't be silly Judy, she said to herself. It's just a coffee and you haven't got anything else to do today.

'Er, yes ok. Do you remember where I live?'

'Oh yes,' he said. 'I drive past it every day. Shall I see you about two-thirty?'

Later that afternoon Judy was sitting opposite Geoff in the small local café that she loved to visit. Eric Clapton Unplugged was playing on repeat as usual but Judy loved it and it added to the makeshift ambience of the café. The other tables were occupied by solitary customers, writing letters, or reading newspapers. The owner took and delivered orders without niceties and left her customers in peace to enjoy their privacy.

Geoff talked about his job as a self-employed computer programmer which sent him far and wide across the southeast region. The travelling could be a pain, but he enjoyed his work as he loved the new technology.

'Have you got a computer, Judy?' Geoff asked. 'If not, I could get you a second-hand one. It would help immensely with your lesson preparation. No more endless sheets of paper and you could experiment with exciting and innovative resources. Your students will love you for it.'

Judy grimaced. In stark contrast to Geoff, she was a Luddite when it came to change, choosing Medieval History in University and centring most of her English classes around grammar and syntax. The nearest she got to technology was an overhead projector and she struggled to cope with that. She didn't want to offend Geoff, so she took the opportunity to veer the subject away from computers and towards her main objective.

'Yes. I've been wanting to upgrade from my pen and paper but haven't known where to start,' she told him. Then before he had a chance to answer, she added, 'What sort of things can you find out about on a computer? It's just that I'm looking for a new place to live and the rooms in the Free Ads papers are usually gone by the time I see the advert.'

'Where are you thinking of moving to?' Geoff asked, with interest. 'I have contacts at a few universities so I'm sure I could find some places for you to look at.'

'Really! Oh, that would be amazing. I promised Chris, I would find us somewhere by the New Year.'

'Chris?'

'Oh yes. Christine. She's my housemate. We are speaking to each other again. I suppose -'

A high-pitched ring tone caused Judy to jump. She looked confused until Geoff reached inside his jacket pocket and removed a mobile phone. Having glanced at the screen he returned it to his pocket.

'That's good.' Suddenly he seemed distracted. 'Thanks for the coffee, Judy. I need to be somewhere now, but can I give you a lift home.'

They had been there less than half an hour and Judy realized she was disappointed to end things so soon. She tried not to show it. Who had phoned him, she wondered? 'No. You go on. I think I'll stay for another coffee.'

'If you are sure. Listen, if you give me your number, I can let you know if I hear about any rooms going.'

Judy quickly scribbled down her phone number on a piece of torn-off menu, before handing it to Geoff. And then he was gone.

London, January 1941

Dear Bertha,

I hope you are safe and well in these troubling times. We met briefly at our cousin Edward's funeral but, unfortunately, my family and I were unable to stay for the Wake.

Forgive us for not contacting you earlier but we assumed that you had moved closer to your sister in Glasgow. However, our solicitor has informed us that you are still living in your house in London and that you are alone. I know that Edward would want us to reach out to you, therefore, I hope you will consider this invitation for you to stay with us, at least until the war is over.

Yours sincerely,

Thomas Lloyd

Chapter Nineteen

Judy was curled up on the settee with a mug of tea when she opened the wooden box for the first time. Inside were several envelopes with letters inside, a few cards, and some newspaper cuttings. Underneath it all was a bundle of old banknotes, five and ten shillings, none of which was still legal tender, but in total it would have been a reasonable sum back in the day. After carefully examining each envelope, she then opened the one that had been on top of the box. It was dated June 1940.

Dear Bertha,

Thank you so much for the money. I cannot tell you how much it is appreciated during this period of hardship. I do not need money beyond paying our rent, bills, and buying food. But James does miss his trips to the pub and cinema.

We do not know how long he is going to be off work, so we are considering letting out our second bedroom. He knows a few people who might be interested, and the money would be handy. It would mean we will lose the guest room but, with Edward away so much, you are unlikely to visit for a while.

Please be careful down there on your own.
Look forward to your next letter.

Yours with love,
Eveline

The letter added a few personal details to the bare bones of Bertha's life. She had a husband but there didn't seem to have been any children at that time. Or maybe Eveline didn't bother to mention them in her letter, though that was unlikely as she mentioned Bertha's husband. And what of Eveline? She and James were obviously struggling for money as they planned to rent out a room.

The other letter had been so poignant, filled with regret and affection for Bertha but it was dated after this letter so circumstances might have changed. Judy wondered why Bertha had been living alone despite being married then she realized that it would have been wartime so he must have been a serving soldier. That probably put him at under forty unless he volunteered. Curious as to his fate she opened the next letter.

Dear Bertha,

We are all so sorry to hear about Edward. He was a very brave man, and we shall always be in his debt. I cannot believe how terrible things have been this past year. I hope you are getting some support from his family though I understand they live quite a distance away.

Unfortunately, we are unable to come to the funeral, as money is tight since James hurt his leg. It is such a long journey. Saving for the fare is almost impossible, what with James being unable to work. He is particularly upset about being deemed medically unfit to join up. It makes him feel so ashamed that Edward was prepared to give his life for our country even though he had such a worthwhile job. James, on the other hand, says he would not be missed by anyone but me.

Hopefully, he will be back working soon, and we can come down for a visit. Then, we can begin to make up for all the years we have spent apart.

Take care dearest sister.

Yours with love,
Eveline

Judy pulled the newspaper cuttings from the bottom of the wooden box and right at the bottom was a Post Office telegram dated June 1940.

REGRET INFORM 691287 EDWARD WILLIAM LLOYD DIED BELGIUM 8 MAY 1940 CONFIRMATION FOLLOWS ARTILLERY RECORDS SIDCUP

So there it was. Poor Bertha's husband was killed in action near the start of the war. That would have left just her in the house without children. She would have held the telegram in her hand just as Judy was at that moment, reading of her husband's death.

Judy was shaken out of her thoughts by the sound of the phone ringing. At first, she was reluctant to answer it as she assumed it was

Christine again. Then she remembered Geoff had her phone number too. She held her breath as she answered it.

'Hello.'

'Hi, Judy. It's Geoff. I think I may have found you somewhere decent to live. If I pick you up in about an hour, we can meet the landlord there.'

'Oh! Okay. I'll be ready.'

An hour later Judy was once again a passenger in Geoff's car. Her damp hair gave off a scent of coconut but only he noticed it. He drove them to a leafy area on the outskirts of east London. It was further away from the college they worked at but was at least near a tube station. He waited in the car while Judy viewed the available rooms. The property was a quaint cottage-style house with three bedrooms, two of which were vacant. The landlord, a university lecturer, was a regular customer of Geoff's. He preferred his tenants to be more mature than the typical student therefore was happy to offer the rooms to Judy and Christine.

'I'm going to give the rooms a lick of paint, and perhaps some new carpet, but they should be ready for you after Christmas.'

It was that easy. He wouldn't take the deposit until the rooms were ready, but he promised Judy she could move in on the 1st of January when the contract would be signed. He would keep the other room for Christine. Before leaving Judy was introduced to the other tenant, Dane, who was stopped on his way out of the front door. The younger man nodded and continued out of the house.

'He's fine, I promise,' the landlord said, laughing. 'I think he likes his privacy though.'

After the success of the morning, Judy and Geoff were soon back in the café that was still playing Eric Clapton Unplugged. This time Geoff insisted on paying for sandwiches as well as coffee. Just as it should be, Judy thought.

He talked about his job travelling around the region, following up appointments which he had made through cold calling potential

152

customers. This part of the job was made easier by his passion for what he was selling. It was a growing industry and he believed he was ahead of the curve which he was able to convey to his customers. He was confident and charming, and Judy could understand why he was successful.

He lived with his two teenage children; his wife having left the previous year. 'We tried to keep things going until both of the kids had left school,' he said, 'but Sue decided she had given them enough of her time so moved in with her boyfriend. It didn't last long so she's now with her parents. The boys are staying with them over Christmas.'

Judy felt embarrassed for Geoff on hearing his story. It must have been difficult for him to admit that his wife had left him for another man. For the first time she saw a weakness in him that she found attractive. While he had been talking she had analysed his features and realized he was a handsome man; tall, slim with dark brown hair and blue eyes. She supposed that he must have found her attractive too as she remembered Reuben's bitter words that a man never makes conversation with a woman unless he is attracted to her. Pushing his estranged family out of her mind, she began to imagine being in a relationship with Geoff and wondered what Christine would make of that.

Then it was her turn. She talked about her teaching job at a private language college; how it was irregular hours but enough to live off. She hoped to increase the hours the following year so that she could afford to rent her own place. Suddenly his eyes glazed over, and she realized how dull her life sounded. Before she could stop herself she invented a long-term plan to teach abroad somewhere, but this she immediately regretted as it sounded just as fanciful as the truth was dull.

His eyes were still glazed over, and she thought he must be wishing he was somewhere else. Then he asked her a question she hadn't been expecting and hadn't prepared herself for.

'What about your family? Do they live locally?'

Judy was quiet for a moment as though wondering what to say. She opened her sandwich and moved the sliced sausage around, then, without any sign of emotion, she spoke.

'Both of my parents are dead.'

Geoff put down his cup and shook his head. 'I'm so sorry Judy. I shouldn't have asked. You don't have to say anything else. We can change the subject.'

'It's alright,' she replied abruptly. 'It was a long time ago and feels like another life somehow. My mother died when I was ten. We were both pushing our car. It was always breaking down. My father was in the driving seat as my mother couldn't drive. Suddenly, she dropped to the floor like a stone. I thought she'd tripped over, so I started to laugh. But she didn't move. My father ran over to us, and I heard him whisper *oh God* to himself. Then he told me to run to the neighbour's house and tell them to call an ambulance. She had some kind of aneurism.'

Interrupted by a woman's arm reaching down to pick up the empty plates, Judy took the chance to compose herself. Then she continued.

'My father refused to talk about it. Before long he had remarried, and I had a stepmother who was only fifteen years older than I was. We moved to a different town where we lived for another five years before my father died of cancer. I was left with my stepmother who didn't take long to remarry herself. They moved once more, and it was made clear that I should go my own way. I was sixteen and too young to rent anywhere so they found me a job as a live-in nanny. I had several jobs after that, living in different towns and cities before I went to university. Somehow I ended up here.'

'That's quite a story,' he said. 'I suppose you don't keep in touch with your stepmother. Why would you after she practically threw you out.'

'It wasn't just her to be fair. I was a nightmare stepdaughter, never accepting her and making it clear I would leave home as soon as I was old enough. I don't think I meant it, at least not until my father died. Anyway, here I am – a real-life Eleanor Rigby.'

Immediately, she regretted that last statement. Why did she always have to bring herself down when she was supposed to be impressing someone. She could see in his eyes that he was probably thinking the same thing. No wonder she had never been in a serious relationship. After an awkward silence, she changed the subject.

'What research can you do on a computer? I want to go to the local library to search for any history of my street. Do you think they will have microfiche or computers? I know microfiche are computers.'

'Not exactly,' he said smiling.

Then just as Judy thought he was going to launch into a lecture on the differences between one heap of glass and plastic and another, he asked her what she wanted to know about the street. He seemed genuinely interested in what she had to say, which, she now knew, was a rarity in a man. So she told him about the letters and how she had a strange need to find out more about Mrs. Bertha Lloyd.

'Are you local Geoff? I remember you saying that you knew the area.'

'No,' he replied, 'but it's well known that this part of the city was bombed heavily during the war, due to its proximity to the industrial sites and its port. I think I'm correct in saying that many hundreds of people were killed in just one night. Records of deaths are kept at St Catherine's House in central London. But you would need a lot more information, such as the approximate birth date and her maiden name.'

Judy sighed as she realized that she didn't have a clue what Bertha's maiden name was. 'How could I find her maiden name?'

'You could start by looking around the local churchyards for her name, or at least her husband's grave. There's a good chance she was buried with him. I'll come with you if you like.' He tilted his head as he smiled, and she blushed and thought that he did too.

'Yes, I'd like that,' she replied.

They agreed it was time to make a move. As she turned towards the door of the cafe, she felt the palm of his hand rest softly on her lower back.

Glasgow, January 1941

It had been raining heavily for days and the river was seeping over its banks. As Eveline walked along the adjacent path, her shoes got wetter and wetter as they stepped into the growing puddles. Every minute or so, a light spray of water would hit the side of her face. She didn't brush it off.

The bank of the River Clyde was a lonely, dangerous place but she was not thinking about that, only what she had learnt this morning; something which had broken her heart. She knew James had followed her out, but she didn't want to talk to him at this moment. Nor could she look at him. She just had to make sense of the things that had happened.

The sound of the river rushing towards the Firth of Clyde, and on towards the sea was deafening. It almost drowned out her sad thoughts. It reminded her of the insignificance of everything that wasn't water or air. Water and air would always be here, she thought. Unlike living creatures like herself, like her parents, like James. Even rocks and soil erode.

Why do people start wars and revolutions when life was so short and meaningless? She remembered the prayers for king and country the children were made to say at St Mary's Orphanage. Yet by the time she was fifteen, the world had already forsaken her, and she felt detached from everything around her. That feeling had returned.

Chapter Twenty

'Maybe she died of a broken heart,' Geoff remarked, without conviction.

'No. Women were stoic back then,' Judy stated, without really knowing if that was true or just a myth.

It had not taken them long to find it - a large granite gravestone engraved with the name,

Edward William Lloyd,
12.12.03 to 13.05.40
beloved husband of Bertha nee Parry,
23.09.07 to 10.05.41

After leaving the café, they had left the car at Judy's house and walked to the nearby Anglican church. The church stood defiant in its solitude. Its crumbling walls looked as neglected as the graves that surrounded them and the absence of any litter did nothing but confirm the lack of visitors. Despite the melancholia which filled the damp air, there was something romantic about it too. Judy imagined the bereaved families throwing earth over their loved ones as they were lowered into the freshly dug ground. Bertha, who had once been as young as her, was buried here too.

For a moment they stood in respectful silence, listening to the sound of a wood pigeon cooing in a nearby willow tree. Then a sudden blast of cold air swept through the graveyard, making Judy shiver. Geoff reached over and grabbed her hand.

'You're freezing. Let's go before you catch your death.'

As they walked back towards the house the wind picked up and Geoff pulled Judy closer to him to shield her from the worst of the weather.

'Shall we run, Judy?' he said, laughing as freezing rain began falling from the darkening sky.

'I'll probably fall over,' she answered, with a smile.

Then he lifted the crook of his arm towards her and said, 'I won't let you fall.'

She threaded her arm into his and they ran until they reached his car, shrieking and laughing as the rain became heavier and heavier.

When they got to his car, he turned to face her once again. 'Are you doing anything on Friday night Judy?' he asked.

Judy's heart began to race. She knew this was the moment she said yes, she was busy that night, but he would know that was a lie. She told him that she hadn't planned anything. Not exactly playing hard to get she thought to herself, but she didn't know how to do things the correct way.

'Would you like to go out to dinner with me? We could make it early evening if you would prefer.'

'Yes,' she answered, surprising herself with her enthusiasm. She hadn't been out on a date for a couple of years and would spend the next couple of days stressing and thinking of reasons to cancel. But at the same time, she was glowing inside.

He didn't make any attempt to kiss her, which was a disappointment, but as they walked back to the car, their arms kept knocking together, fleeting physical contact that neither tried to prevent. When they got to his car, he turned to face her once again.

'I'll see you Friday evening Judy.' Then, he smiled warmly, got into his car, and drove away.

She hadn't asked him in for coffee but there was no need. They were already connected. Her life had changed in a matter of a few minutes, and she couldn't have been happier. Could it be that she wasn't facing life on her own anymore?

Judy watched Geoff's car disappearing before she shut the front door. It had been one of those standoff moments. Who was going to turn away first? Finally, after waiting for her to unlock the door and step inside the house, he'd waved and slowly driven away. It had been a day too perfect to seem real, and she still found it difficult to believe it had happened. She found herself dancing around the kitchen, holding the kettle like it were a baby when there was a knock at the door. It was Reuben.

'Sorry to bother you, Judy, but I just needed to apologise for my behaviour the other day. I haven't been able to stop thinking about it.'

'There's no need for you to apologise, Reuben,' she answered nervously. 'It was nothing, just a silly misunderstanding, that's all.'

'Please, could I come in and explain. I promise I'll keep away from you.' His words were coherent, yet his eyes were desperate. Judy felt sorry for him.

'Yes, of course. I'll make some tea.'

A few minutes later Reuben was sitting opposite Judy, staring into his mug of tea, as though entranced by the bits of stale milk swirling around on top.

'Things have been stressful at home lately. My mother is very unwell.'

'I'm sorry.'

'Mentally unwell, that is. She has a kind of dementia whereby she isn't always aware of her surroundings. Sometimes she thinks she is a little girl again and doesn't know who I am.'

'That must be really upsetting for you, Reuben.'

'Yes…yes, it is,' he replied, his voice quivering. 'The doctors say that it could be a genetic disorder but can't be certain as her mother died during the war.'

Judy watched Reuben as he stared down at his tea and waited quietly for him to continue. For the first time he looked older than his years. His mother was clearly a heavy burden on him.

Finally, he lifted his eyes to meet hers. 'That day she had rung me at work and was hysterical, screaming for her mother. It wasn't the first time, but I just couldn't handle it that day. I needed to get out of my world for a while…into someone else's world.'

'But you helped me, Reuben. I would never have got my car if it weren't for you. And I wanted you to look around the house. You just weren't yourself, that's all. No harm done.'

'That's kind of you to say, Judy. I really appreciate it.' His eyes looked tired.

'Isn't there anyone else who could help you? Brothers? Sisters? What about your fath…' she stopped herself as she remembered he had never mentioned any other family members.

'No. I'm an only child. My parents had me late in life and my father died ten years ago. But he wasn't that much of a help when he was alive. Anyway, thanks for listening. I'd better get back.' He put down his undrunk tea and stood up. Without looking at Judy, he walked down the hall and out of the house that he no longer seemed aware of.

As she said goodbye and closed the door after him, Judy made an early New Year's resolution to be more considerate towards Reuben. Remembering what he had said about his grandmother dying in the war, her thoughts returned to Bertha. Her year of death was 1941 so she could have been killed in the bombings, rather than died of natural causes. She walked into her bedroom and opened the wooden box.

For the first time, she noticed a tiny box amongst the notes and letters, the type that jewellery was placed in when bought. She picked it up and opened the lid to see a gold locket on a delicate chain. On examination she saw that it was hallmarked, and inside were two tiny photographs of girls. There were a few years between them. The younger girl wore a pale bonnet that framed her chubby face. The older girl had lost the puppy fat, her sharper features exposed by her tied-back dark hair.

Judy realized that this must be the locket mentioned in the letter she had found on the stairs, the one that had seemed so poignant. Although that was the first letter she had read, it must have been one of the last ones written. Bertha had clearly cherished the locket as Eveline had hoped she would.

Judy looked again at the photograph of Eveline in 1941 standing alone by the sideboard. She wondered why there were no photographs of the husbands, even though, according to her first letter, Eveline had sent one. Perhaps it had been framed and then lost over the years. Or maybe her family, wherever they were, had kept the photographs as heirlooms. She wondered if both sides of the family were still in touch or if there had been any descendants. It was clear that Eveline was very unhappy, possibly due to a childless marriage and her husband being out of work. Her words painted a picture of a life filled with regret. The contents of the box brought a lump to Judy's throat. Now she felt more determined to pass all the letters, the photograph, and the locket onto Bertha's family, if they still existed.

Judy felt an affinity with the two sisters, which she rarely felt with her contemporaries. How old would they be today, she wondered? Ninety? Ninety-five? She remembered the woman called Iris in the care home. What year did she say she was born? Perhaps they had known each other. Maybe she would ask her, even show her the photograph to see if she recognised Eveline. Wasn't it the case that long-term memory never faded? Although she had forgotten the last few years, Iris still remembered her younger days, so it was worth a try. She would make another trip to the home when Becky got back from her parents. She picked up another letter but, surprised by the different register, wondered if Bertha and Eveline had fallen out in between.

It was dated 20th April 1941.

Dear Bertha,

Thank you for your last letter. James and I are both well. We hope you are too. I am sorry it has been some time since I last wrote to you but there has been a big change in our lives. Last month I had a baby whom we have given the name Stanley.

This must come as much of a surprise to you, as it has to us. We had long given up our hope of children after I suffered many losses, but we have finally been blessed.

Stanley is quite a handful and takes up my entire day so it will not be easy to respond to your letters as quickly as before. However, I look forward to reading them all the same.

I will write again as soon as I can.

Yours,
Eveline

So Eveline had had a child after all. It must have been quite late for a firstborn, she thought, especially in those days. Looking again at the woman in the photograph, Judy tried to imagine her in more modern clothes and decided she could probably pass for mid-thirties rather than forties. She certainly didn't look pregnant in the photograph so it must have been taken at least a month or two after the birth. But then Stanley being a handful may have burnt off the baby fat quicker than usual. It was more than likely the child was still alive somewhere, possibly still living in Glasgow. Of course, he could be the landlord, and, if so, finding him would be easier than she had thought. She could ask Russell for his contact details when she next saw him.

There was only one letter left to read. The last letter was very brief and clearly in response to another letter from Bertha, dated 5th May 1941.

Dear Bertha,

There is no need for you to visit us. It was going to be a surprise but as we have arranged to come down to you on Saturday afternoon.

Look forward to seeing you.
Eveline

Judy wondered if Eveline and James still came down as it must have been a difficult journey during wartime, made harder with a young baby. Why would they make such a journey during the Blitz? Surely it would have been safer to let Bertha travel up to them unless the bombing was just as bad up there. Where exactly was 'up there' though as Glasgow was a huge city? She made a mental note to go through the envelopes once again to check the post marks.

She read it again paying attention to the day of the planned visit, Saturday. That must have been extremely close to the date of Bertha's death which she remembered was in May, May 10[th.] Could they have been here when Bertha died? Maybe it was during an air raid. Or perhaps she had been struck down with a sudden illness. For now, she decided to take a trip to the local library. There she would see if there were any records about the area for that period. Hopefully, there would be reports about where the bombs had fallen and if many residents had been killed. Perhaps there would be a mention of Bertha.

Glasgow, April 1941

James and Dot looked at each other when they saw the envelope in the hallway. It was another letter from Bertha. James picked up the envelope, tore it open and took out the sheet of paper inside. After reading the words aloud, he knew they would have to settle things once and for all.

'I have to tell her something,' James said calmly, 'before she contacts the police. We don't know where all this could end.

Dot nodded but didn't answer. Silently she wondered if she should get away while she still had the chance. But she knew she had nowhere else to go. No family. No friends. James and Eveline were the only people she knew, and she didn't even know them very well.

'Do you want me to come with you James?' she asked, hoping he would say no. He did.

'What would be the point of that Dot? Unless you pretend to be Eveline, it would just be a waste of a train ticket, and I can barely afford my own.'

'Are you going to tell her the truth?' she asked. Once again she considered the idea of not being there when he returned from London.

'I don't know what I'll tell her,' he muttered. 'I'll decide when I get there. I have no idea what she looks like, what sort of woman she is, how she is likely to react. It's been so many years since she and Eveline were last together, I dare say they wouldn't even recognize each other.'

He walked over to the kitchen shelf and took down a small tin which rattled when he opened it. He counted the shillings and pound notes inside, took most out, then replaced the tin.

'There is just enough for the return fare and a bit left over for groceries. You'll have to manage until I come back.'

'If you come back,' she thought.

165

Chapter Twenty-one

At the library Judy settled down in front of one of the new computers that had recently been installed in the research room. The librarian had given her a disc to insert into the computer and, after a bit of help, a list of newspapers came up on the screen. She would only need one from 1941 to work out the exact date of Eveline and James's proposed visit. But once she started to read the first paper she couldn't stop.

The first report was from September 1940. It stated that London was bombed for eight and a half hours, which saw several buses and a hospital hit. There was none of the emotive language that modern journalism excelled at, nor heart-wrenching images of women and children crying amongst the bodies of loved ones. In fact, there were no pictures at all, just details of times and places of attacks. But however bad it had been, Bertha had survived that raid.

She moved forward to another report from a couple of weeks before Bertha's death. This time the objective behind the journalism was more than to merely report the news. The front pages were filled with photographs of bombed-out houses, women trudging through the rubble, sandbags propping up walls, and Winston Churchill looking defiant. This was the Blitz spirit that the older generation always lectured the young about. Defiance in the face of death.

Judy wondered why anyone would make a nonessential visit during such a time of turmoil. The journey would have taken all day. She did a mental calculation then sat back in the chair. Would Saturday have been the date of Bertha's death? She looked for a newspaper for the days following that Saturday and she found exactly what she was looking for.

The front page of a local paper showed The House of Commons on fire, crashed planes bearing the Swastika, and the words 'thousands feared dead in London's longest night. The newspaper was dated 12th May 1941. The date of Betha's death was May 10th, 1941, so she must have died in that bombing. It was even possible that Eveline, James, and the baby had died too given they had planned to be with Bertha in London. Or had they changed their minds about coming down?

Next she looked at the Scottish newspapers to see whether Glasgow had in any way suffered the same fate as the South. It had. Just a couple of nights after the London bombing, the 'Clydebank Blitz' had killed twelve hundred people. She looked in an atlas and found where Clydebank was in relation to Glasgow. It was close enough. What if Eveline's family were killed during that bomb attack?

Judy racked her brain to think of a way she could find out if they had outlived Bertha. Then she had another idea. She went to the section of the library which kept telephone directories for other parts of the country, taking out those that covered the Glasgow area. She knew Eveline and James's surname and they'd had a baby boy so his name wouldn't have changed. It was a long shot but was all she could think of. So she settled down with a pen and paper. On her way home she called at the post office to change a five-pound note into ten and twenty pence pieces.

An hour after she had got home Judy's list of names had three crossed out, four with N.A for no answer, and two with questions marks – those that had answered but hung up in confusion. Judy was struggling to understand the Glaswegian accent, and they could barely hear her Welsh lilt. Perhaps this had not been such a good idea and there was a better way of dealing with the issue.

Then she had another idea. She could write each person a letter instead, as their addresses were also in the telephone directory. It would be easier to explain in writing. She would mention what she knew about Eveline and James, Bertha and Edward, and the baby of course. She could also mention Dot, who could still possibly be alive. She had less than two weeks before she moved out so she would also give the cottage address in case they did not reply straight away; that's if they replied at all.

She would also send for a death certificate for Bertha now that she had her maiden name and date of death. It would only take a few days to get it back. It might include the cause of death, but she wasn't sure. What had it said on her parent's death certificates? She couldn't remember if she had ever seen the certificates. If they still existed, her stepmother would have them, and Judy doubted she was the type to hold onto them. She hadn't even paid for a gravestone for her father. It was as though her parents had never existed. No stone or paper preserving their memory, just their daughter. But that wasn't the past that mattered right now.

Dear Mr/Mrs/ Miss Preece,

I am trying to trace the family of Stanley Preece, born in Glasgow in the early part of 1941. I have in my possession several items which I would like to pass onto him. These include a collection of letters from his mother, Eveline to her sister, Bertha, some photographs, and a locket. I came across them while renting a room at 12 Market Road, London, and would like to give them to Bertha's closest family member, who I have reason to believe is Stanley.

There is also a letter from a Thomas Lloyd in Hampshire who I believe was a relative of her husband, Edward.

If you are not the Stanley Preece that I am looking for please disregard this letter and accept my apologies.

Yours sincerely,

Judy Snow

Her letter was short and to the point, as she had to write it over twenty times. There was just enough time to write the letters, address the envelopes and run to the post office to buy stamps before the last post of the day. Once that was done she would put the box back into the attic cupboards and forget about it for a few days at least. She would think of nothing other than her date with Geoff the following evening.

The menu was written in French. Confit de Canard. Coquilles Saint-Jaques. Boeuf Bourguignon - ah, that was something she recognised.

'I'll have the beef borginon,' she announced, to the smirking waiter.

'I'll have the same,' Geoff added, before handing back his menu.

'So, we were taught German at my school,' she said defensively.

Geoff laughed. 'Who does know how to pronounce Beef Bourguignon? Probably not even French people.'

'Apart from waiters, of course.'

Both diners, orders completed, rested back in their seats to face each other. There was a relaxed atmosphere between them though there had been an awkward moment when the waiter had recommended oysters as hors d'oeuvres. Hearing only the word

169

huitres, Judy had glanced at Geoff for guidance, but he'd gently shaken his head muttering something about a first date. They settled for the smoked salmon canapes. From that point the conversation flowed effortlessly.

'I must have walked past this restaurant dozens of times, yet I've never noticed it before,' she said while unconsciously running her left hand through her freshly washed hair.

'It is slightly off the beaten track, but I came across it during one of my selling crusades. They didn't buy a computer though.'

'How did you get into that line of work?'

'I've always been a bit of a computer nerd, to be honest. Where my friends had Hornby train sets and Air fix models, I would be taking apart my Nintendo games, much to my parents' horror. After finishing my electronics degree at college, sales seemed the ideal job for keeping on top of progress. Sorry. This must be boring for you.'

'Not at all. You must be close to being a genius if you can understand how computers work. I struggle to change a fuse.'

'That's because changing a fuse is a man's job,' he replied, with a grin.

'Yes. The Pankhurst sisters have a lot to answer for.'

They both laughed barely noticing the waiter who stood patiently holding their smoked salmon canapes. For the next couple of hours, they were in their own private space, oblivious of their fellow diners, fascinated with each other's conversation. Then it was time to leave, and they began the long walk home.

'I feel guilty for not driving, 'he said, as he watched her pulling her coat tightly around her body.

'Well, don't because I absolutely insisted, if you remember. I was certainly not going to drink while you sat there sober.'

It had been agreed that the substantial meal, along with the long walk home, should be enough to clear the alcohol out of Geoff's system. The police were certain to be out in force on a night so close to Christmas and with so many drunken revellers around the streets. But he'd only had a couple of drinks during the evening.

'What are you going to do over Christmas, Judy?'

'Watch dozens of blockbuster movies while munching my way through a tin of Quality Streets.'

There was silence for a minute. He put his arm around her shoulders and kissed the top of her head.

'You are quite special; you know that don't you.'

It was such an intimate gesture and she dealt with it in her clumsy way, by bringing someone else into the moment. 'It must be difficult for you too, with your wife... you know,'

'Oh, we'll get through it somehow. It's only a couple of days after all.'

They reached the church in which Bertha and her husband were buried and stopped as though to pay their respects. Then their attention turned to the notice board.

'When both my parents were alive we always went to Midnight Mass,' Judy said sadly. Then, she laughed. 'It was the only time I got to stay up that late.'

Geoff did not laugh. Instead, he replied, 'We could go together if you like?'

When they finally reached the iron gate in front of the house, Judy continued walking up to the front door. Before she put the key in the lock, he gently took her arm and turned her to face him.

'May I just thank you for your wonderful company tonight. I'm looking forward to a reunion on Christmas Eve?' He smiled.

'Yes. I'd like that very much.' She smiled back, shyly. 'Well, thanks again.'

She leant over to kiss him on the cheek, but he moved his head slightly to meet her lips. For what seemed like an eternity the two embraced, neither wanting to be the first to pull back. Eventually, she did.

'Do you want to come in for ...'

'Better not.'

He walked down the path and towards his car, looking back to wave as he opened the door. Once again he waited until Judy had gone inside before he drove away. Judy stayed leaning against the front door until it became too cold to enjoy the moment. It was a moment like nothing she'd experienced in her life.

It was still quite early so the streets were not yet filled with drunken revellers. Driving so soon after the wine had been a risk even though Geoff felt sure he was still under the legal limit. He could have stayed yet the time was just not right. He would wait until Christmas Day. As his car turned off the main road into the cul de sac he noticed that a light was on in the upstairs bedroom. He knew he hadn't left it on. His heart sank.

London, May 10th, 1941

Susan Carson walked away from her front door on tip toe. She was taking no chances. He usually slept for a few hours after his tea, sozzled as he was from the beer that he'd drunk in the Arms beforehand. It had not been so easy with her young daughter who was terrified of the bombs. But Susan told her she was going to fetch a present for her father and promised she would be back soon.

'Remember it's our little secret, Joan,' she had whispered to her.

Please don't look out now, she whispered at the neighbour's window, as she crept past it wheeling her bicycle. Her neighbour always left the front room curtains open with the light switched off as if passers-by wouldn't notice her standing in the dark room. Noisy old bat she thought, turning her head away to face the other side of the road. If the neighbour only saw her once she should assume that Susan was going to post a letter. However, she would probably be gone at least an hour, so she had to make sure she wasn't seen returning. It would be very awkward trying to explain an hour-long absence if this was raised over their back-garden wall chat the next morning.

Fortunately, there was little sign that Susan had been seen. The curtains were as still as the darkness of the room: no twitching, no shadows, no peering eyes. She started to walk faster now that she was out of sight, working out the schedule in her mind. Ten minutes to get there; thirty minutes there; ten, maybe twenty minutes to get home. She might have to leave her bicycle there. And Susan could be home in bed before her husband woke up, and he never bothered her on a Sunday night. Then she would never let him touch her again.

Chapter Twenty-two

Even without decorations there was a Christmas atmosphere in the house. It wasn't too late. However, rather than unravelling Christmas tree lights, Judy was putting everything into the chicken casserole she was cooking. Geoff wasn't due until seven-thirty, so it gave her the chance to enjoy a sneaky glass of wine in front of the television. As she watched the choir dressed in white and red robes announcing the arrival of Christmas, she mulled over the recent change in her life.

It would have been fun to share her experiences with others but there was no one else. Becky had taken two weeks' leave over the Christmas holidays and disappeared to her parent's house. Christine had also returned to her family for a two-week break. It was, of course, traditional for families to congregate at that time, to share precious time with parents and siblings. The problem was Judy had no family. She tried not to let Christmas be the difficult time of year that everyone assumed it was for 'the lonely'.

In the past, she had thrown herself into the voluntary soup-kitchen experience which enabled the lonely volunteers to count their blessings in the face of the homeless. She had visited elderly men and women whose families either lived too far away to visit, or just couldn't be bothered. Those visits were not so rewarding as the elderly often ended up forgetting their own woes and feeling sorry for Judy. 'Is that your life?' an old woman had exclaimed once when Judy had described a typical week.

So eventually she gave up the self-sacrifice that the spirit of Christmas demanded and allowed herself to wallow in three days of nuts, crisps, chocolates, and wine. But this year everything was going to be so different. This year there would be Geoff.

The phone rang.

'Hello, Judy.' It was Geoff and his voice was unusually quiet.

'Hi Geoff,' she replied excitedly, assuming the line was poor. 'You only just caught me as I was just getting into the shower. That's why I took so long to answer. Are you still okay for seven-thirty?'

There was silence for a few seconds and for a moment she thought he'd been cut off. Then he spoke. 'Judy. I'm sorry but I must cancel our meeting later. I hope that you haven't gone to any trouble.'

'Oh.' Her voice betrayed the disappointment she felt on hearing his words. 'That's alright. Are you unwell? I can come over to you if -'

'No.' It was almost a shout. 'I shan't be able to see you again. My wife has come home, and we have agreed to make another go of things for the sake of the children.'

'But what about me,' she said. 'I thought you liked me, Geoff.' It sounded pathetic and she wished she could take the words back the second they left her mouth.

'I do like you Judy, but we could never be more than friends. I'm sorry if I gave you the wrong idea.'

'Er, actually, yes you did give me the wrong idea. Taking me out to dinner. Telling me not to worry about your wife as the marriage was over.' Judy was shocked at her own caustic tone and wished that she had not reacted so emotionally. 'Are you sure this is what you want, Geoff?' she asked, her voice softening.

But before Geoff had a chance to answer, the pips went and there was no sound of any more coins dropping. Was he even listening to her? Then the tone that signalled the end of the connection came through the receiver. She replaced it and stared at it for the following ten minutes, willing it to ring again. Perhaps he didn't have any more change, or his wife was with him, and that is why he referred to their date as a meeting.

A feeling of insecurity engulfed her as she reviewed the conversation leading up to his asking her out to dinner. Did she misread his intentions, or had he merely been playing with her emotions? On the other hand, she had not exactly played hard to get, and weren't men supposed to like a chase. Suddenly realizing she was standing in the hallway half-dressed, she returned to the bathroom and put her jeans back on. Time to drown her sorrows.

The bottle lay empty on the coffee table in front of Judy who was leafing through the Yellow Pages. The back door was open and most of the smoke had cleared. How was it even possible for a burnt casserole to cause so much carnage? Now she was starving, and it would have to be dial-a-pizza. She staggered over to the telephone and dialled the takeaway number. While waiting for an answer she noticed Geoff's card on top of the phone box, and she jotted down his phone number on her hand. He had only given her his home number but not his address. Maybe she could find it.

After ordering her pizza, she picked up the residential telephone directory and took it into the sitting room. Within the last couple of hours, she had gone from the excitement of preparing for a dinner date to scouring through the phone book looking for a man's address.

There were hundreds of entries under the name G Thomas but only one with his number of course. He had given her his home telephone number, wife or not. She drew an asterisk next to his address in the telephone book. The area was unfamiliar, but she would find it. He couldn't have suddenly gone off her just because his wife turned up, and she was sure to leave him again anyway. Judy would make sure she told him that in case he was in denial. His wife didn't love him anymore and he didn't love his wife. If he still loved his wife, he wouldn't have asked Judy out. She had to make him see that, and tomorrow she would.

Judy was shaken out of her thoughts by the sound of the doorbell ringing. It made her heart jump so much it hurt. That had to be Geoff. He must have changed his mind when he heard her voice down the telephone. They had a connection that could not be denied. It was as if fate had sent her to the service station and led her to park her car next to those young yobs.

Her hand was shaking as she struggled to open the door. The pizza delivery man stood in front of her with a large bag. He looked cross when he saw she had no money with her even though she knew he was coming. Tears streamed down her face as she fumbled around in her bag for the money and once again the pizza man frowned as she tipped a pile of silver coins into his outstretched hand. Judy, however, cared nothing about his disapproval. She had lost her appetite in the few minutes that had given her both renewed hope and heartache.

As she closed the door, she caught sight of someone standing across the road from the house. They seemed to be looking at her, but it was probably her imagination. Was it a man or a woman? She didn't care. It wasn't Geoff. He wasn't coming and she had never felt so miserable.

That night Judy dreamt she was walking along the pavement of a road that resembled that of one of her childhood addresses. In the dream she was barefoot and aware of the cold hard tarmac beneath her small tender feet. When she reached her destination, she saw it was indeed the house in which she had lived as a little girl, an image she had long forgotten. She knocked at the door, but no one answered so she opened it and entered. Then she climbed up the wooden stairs into her bedroom.

For a moment she couldn't remember why she was there but when she saw her naked feet, she began to look for a pair of shoes. She began to search through a pile of shoes in an old, heavy wardrobe that was too large for her little bedroom. Then she looked through a second wardrobe. However, there was only one of each type of shoe; one trainer, one sandal, one boot. The only shoes in pairs were satin heels and silver dancing shoes all of which were far too sophisticated for her.

Next she went into her parent's bedroom where she saw her mother sitting on the bed; but the bed had two mattresses on it. Her mother looked different from how Judy remembered her, smaller and paler. But it was her mother, and she was happy that she was still alive.

'Where have you been?' Judy asked her. 'I've missed you so much.' But her mother did not answer.

Then her father was standing at Judy's side and asked her why she was there.

'I'm looking for my shoes, Dad, but I can't find them anywhere.'

He smiled and told her that she did not need her shoes where she was going.

Her pillow was wet when she opened her eyes. Even her sleep depressed her. Then she was angry. Not angry at Geoff, or Christine. She was just angry at herself for being so eager to care about people who didn't really give her a second thought. Throwing back the duvet she stepped onto the bedroom floor and picked up the wooden box. A few minutes later she was standing in the dark attic room. It was time to move on.

Part Two

Chapter Twenty-three

'Could she have gone on holiday?' asked the portly female police officer, standing behind the glassed front desk.

'Well, no,' Christine insisted. 'She would have left me a note or something and she has my parent's phone number so she could easily have phoned me in France. In fact, she rang me there to give me our new address. We were due to move into our new house share. She was supposed to move in a few days before I did but she hasn't been near the house. There was no one else in the house over Christmas, just her, so someone may have broken in.'

'Have you contacted her family?'

'I don't know who to contact. I think she was estranged from her close family. She never mentioned anyone else.'

'Does she have a boyfriend?'

'No. She doesn't bother with men, or women for that matter. She never goes out, just to work. Occasionally she comes out with my other friends and me, but usually I leave her on her own. I don't think she is interested in other people, to be honest. She is not a very sociable person. I'm possibly the only person who knows her now.'

'Do you think she's a possible suicide risk then?'

Christine gasped at the mention of the word. She had never considered Judy to be the depressed type, just anti-social. 'Oh my, I didn't until I just described her. I suppose she is quite a sad figure, bit of a loner.'

'And you are certain she isn't still at,' looking at her notes, '12 Market Road?'

'Yes. I've told you. The young man that let us the rooms was there when I got back. He told me all her things were gone and the house was unoccupied.'

'Do you think she could have gone on holiday herself, with the money that you gave her? Perhaps she met someone while you were away. And she probably had a spare pair of glasses. Most people do. There are all sorts of possibilities, so I'd try not to worry yet.'

Christine could sense that the direction of the conversation was moving away from her, and she showed her frustration by shouting,

'You don't understand. You have never met her. I know her. I know what she would and wouldn't do and she would not leave without telling me.'

The brief display of emotion did not affect the policewoman behind the desk. 'I'm afraid there is not a lot we can do at this point in time. She isn't due back to work for another few days so she could be anywhere. She is a fully grown woman and you don't seem to know her all that well. If she hasn't shown up in a week, come back and we'll look further into it.'

Christine left the police station unsatisfied. She got the impression that the police officer did not take this seriously and wouldn't at least for the next couple of weeks. But for Christine, it would remain on her conscience until she found her. She knew she had a responsibility as the only person who knew the circumstances around Judy's disappearance. Christine had laughed at the thought of Judy being on her own in that horrible house for three weeks but now she felt ashamed as she imagined how frightening it must have been for her. If the shoe were on the other foot, would she forgive Judy for forgetting about her?

There was a chance everything was alright, of course. Maybe Judy would turn up in college on Monday. That would be rather awkward, but still a relief. What reason would she give for her absence and failure to complete the move? But there would be no reason, and Christine had a grave feeling that there was something sinister about her housemate's disappearance.

Sure enough Judy wasn't in college when Christine started back the following week. Suzanna, the manager of the private college, was as much in the dark as Christine, though she was far more annoyed than she was concerned. Judy's classes had to be cancelled that day and without the protection of a contract, she would be lucky to keep her job, even if she did eventually show up.

Reuben, however, showed plenty of concern and demanded answers to what Christine thought were ridiculous questions. Had she contacted Judy's family Did Judy leave a note? Had Christine been to the police? While asking those questions he stared deep into Christine's eyes as though he were a detective interrogating a murder suspect. He certainly didn't resemble the nervous Reuben from before the holidays - the Reuben who clearly couldn't wait to get Christine out of his car. Was he blaming her for something that had happened while she was away? Had Judy moaned to him about her? What could she possibly have told him?

Christine found herself getting flustered and tripping over her words which was ridiculous, so she turned to walk away. But as she expected, Reuben called after her.

'Christine. What are you going to do next?'

She turned back to face him. 'I haven't a clue, but I will do something. I'm not going to pretend that this is normal behaviour.'

Before she turned away again, she asked him, 'Will you help me look for her?'

So Christine found herself in the passenger seat of the old Morris 1000 which, once again, was taking her home. She hadn't been desperate for a lift home as it was still light, but Reuben insisted this time. Shortly after, sitting at the kitchen table and nursing a coffee that he didn't intend to drink, Reuben went over his previous conversation with Judy. He recalled how she had talked about the house being haunted.

'She was quite nervous about staying here on her own so I wouldn't be surprised if she did move out earlier than planned,' he said.

'But that doesn't explain where she is now,' Christine insisted. 'She wouldn't give up her job just like that.'

'Had you argued before you left for Christmas?' Reuben's interrogative tone had reappeared. This time Christine's own tone was defensive but firm.

'Of course we argued sometimes but never seriously. I'm sure you have arguments at home occasionally. Anyway, we were fine the night I left, and I even trusted her with my deposit. What if we go back to the new house to see if she's turned up there?'

'I don't see any point in doing that,' he replied. 'You said the rooms had been rented out to other people and she never even moved in there. If in the unlikely event she did go back there, it doesn't explain why she didn't come to work today No. That's a dead end. I think the first thing we need to do is speak to this Russell. He might remember something else that is important. It sounds as though he was the last person to see her, apart from you of course.'

Christine looked unconvinced. 'I don't know where Russell is living now, and he won't call around until Friday. I'll be at work all day, so I won't be able to catch him. I might not see him for weeks.'

'Then don't leave him any rent and he will be sure to look for you,' Reuben told her. 'As soon as he sees that empty cupboard, he'll be all over you. Let's have a good look in her old room for now. Maybe we'll find something between those two mattresses.'

He walked down the hallway and entered the room second door from the front. Christine followed him into the room which looked virtually the same as it had before Judy moved into it. It was as if the last few months had not happened, and Judy had never been in this house. Christine knew deep down there was nothing to be found but went through the motions of searching thoroughly, although this was merely a matter of stripping down the bedclothes and lifting the two mattresses.

As she had thought, there was nothing of interest to be found and they both agreed to call it a day. They would see if anything had changed by the time they met at work in the morning.

Later, Christine thought about Reuben and how he had gone straight to Judy's room as if he already knew where it was. Judy must have told him quite a lot about her room. He even knew about the two mattresses which she thought was an odd thing for Judy to disclose to him. She wondered if Reuben was being totally honest with her and if he had been in the house before, and even in Judy's room. He did seem to be overly concerned about a woman he barely knew Perhaps something had happened between them while she had been away, she thought. But why didn't he just say? Unless he didn't want anyone to know.

After he had left she noticed a letter on the hall floor, hidden beneath the junk mail. The date on the stamp was marked 27th December so it must have been lying there for at least a week. How had she missed it? When she saw the name on the envelope, she wasn't sure about opening it as she had a feeling it was a criminal offence to open someone else's post. On reflection she decided it was her only lead and she steamed open the envelope that was addressed to Judy.

There was no letter inside, just an odd-looking piece of paper. On closer examination she saw the name, Bertha Lloyd. It was a death certificate. Who on earth was Bertha Lloyd, she wondered, and why did Judy want her death certificate? Was she a relative of Judy's? The woman died in 1941, without issue, so Judy couldn't be her direct descendant, at least not in wedlock. Nothing made sense. The date of this letter added to the mystery as it suggested that Judy expected to still be there when it arrived.

Reuben was right about Russell. When Christine didn't leave her rent in the cupboard, she came home to find the young man lying on the settee watching television.

'Oh, Russell, I'm so sorry. I completely forgot to leave the rent this morning, but I've got it here in my bag.'

'No problem,' he said, while switching the television off with the remote control.

'Russell.'

'Yeah.'

'Do you know somebody called Bertha Lloyd?'

Russell appeared to be really surprised at the question, but Christine was even more surprised by his answer.

'Yeah. She was a great aunt of mine. Lived here years ago. Why do you ask?'

'But I thought you didn't know the family who owns this house,' Christine said, trying not to sound critical.

If Russell had picked up any critical tone in her voice, he did not show it. 'Yeah, I know. I didn't want other tenants to feel uneasy about me living here too. So I just pretended to be another renter. How did you find out about her anyway? She's been dead, like, forever.'

This was the trickiest part for Christine; should she admit to opening Judy's post? She decided she had little choice; however, she embellished her version of events.

'I saw a letter in the hallway and thought it was for me, so I opened it. When I saw what it was, I checked the envelope and Judy's name was on it.'

'And what was it?'

'It was your great aunt's death certificate,' she replied, realizing how bizarre it must have sounded to him. She had just taken it as another strange event in the ongoing mystery of Judy's disappearance, but he could be really freaked out by it. She decided to deflect from that by asking more questions about Bertha. 'Russell, did Bertha have any children?'

Russell, however, did not respond for a few seconds. Instead, he looked as though he was thinking about something and not listening anymore. Then he said, 'Ah, I remember her saying something about finding a letter from my grandmother to Bertha. I thought it was a bit weird her being so interested in them seeing that she didn't know them. I think she had too much time on her hands. I'd forgotten about it till now. Anyway, I gotta go. Can I have the rent?'

Christine took the rent money out of her bag while wondering whether to continue questioning Russell. She knew she might not see him again for a while, so she repeated her last question.

Russell shook his head. 'No, she and her husband were both killed in the war, during the Blitz, I think. My grandmother was her only relative, so the house passed to her. She never wanted to leave Scotland so always rented it out.'

'Do you want to have it?' she asked him, while holding out the death certificate.

For a few seconds, he looked confused. 'Have what? Oh, that! No. Just chuck it.'

London, 10th May 1941

Susan knocked nervously on the door of 12 Market Road before it was opened by Bertha, who showed her inside. After telling Susan to leave her bicycle in the hallway, Bertha led her upstairs to the front room. She was shocked when Susan took off her coat and she saw her swollen belly.

'Why have you waited until now?' Bertha asked critically. She hadn't performed an abortion at such a late stage, and she knew it would add to the risk of something going wrong.

'Please help me. I can't go through with this again,' the pregnant woman sobbed. 'The last few weeks have been hell for me. I've tried my hardest but the longer I leave it the more I want to die. If you don't help me, I shall kill myself.'

'What about your husband? Does he know you are here?'

'No. He doesn't even know I'm pregnant. We've already a daughter so he wouldn't be bothered. I haven't told anyone I'm here; I promise.'

Bertha had seen desperation like Susan's when she was a nurse at the local medical practice where she met her husband. A young, teenage girl had begged and begged for her husband, a general practitioner, to abort her early pregnancy. But it was against the law. He advised her to tell her parents and suggested that her mother could bring the child up as her own. Finally, the teenage girl had agreed to tell her parents and she left the surgery quietly. The following day they heard she had jumped in front of an underground train. It haunted both her and her husband. She told Susan to lie down on the mattress.

Chapter Twenty-four

Hearing a knock at the front door, Christine tried to identify the dark figure behind the frosted glass, well at least identify their purpose. The postman? A policeman? She could tell it wasn't Gary, Reuben, or Russell as the shape was too short, and her friends had never been anywhere near the house. She braced herself for the surprise. On opening the door, she was met with the face of a youngish woman. The woman was pretty in a plain way, with thick glasses enlarging her eyes, and her brown hair swept up in a bun. She had a gothic style of dress; long and black, to counter the dullness of her upper body appearance. Christine had never seen her before.

The caller appeared to consider Christine before she finally spoke. 'Hello. Is Judy there? I was just passing, and I thought -'

'Judy?' replied a confused Christine.

'I'm sorry. Have I got the wrong house? Judy told me it was Market Road, but I forgot the number. Her car is outside though so perhaps she lives next door.'

'What! Her car is outside!' Christine pushed past the bemused visitor. There was a car outside, but it wasn't Judy's, just the same colour of a common make and model.

'No, you are not right. That is not Judy's car. The number plate is different,' she explained. 'And you won't find her next door either.'

The woman was now looking over Christine's shoulder certain that she was at the correct address, despite being mistaken about the car.

Christine stirred herself from her confusion. She had absolutely no idea who the woman was but there must be some connection with Judy. 'Yes, she did live here, I mean does live here. Do you want to come in?'

The woman followed Christine through the hallway into the sitting room, looking around her with owl-like flexibility. 'It's not what I was expecting. Why do you keep mattresses in the hall?'

Not worrying about rudeness, Christine had no time to answer such trivial questions. 'Judy's not here. In fact, she hasn't been here for several weeks. Who exactly are you?'

'I'm her old college friend, Becky. We bumped into each other sometime before Christmas. I did promise to call around, but you know how things are?'

'She never mentioned you,' snapped Christine. The brittleness of the answer caused the other woman to raise both eyebrows at once, stretching her eyes in a way that bore yet more resemblance to an owl. This had the effect of making Christine apologise like a pupil who had been impertinent towards her teacher. She wondered if Becky was a teacher. 'I'm sorry but things have been very strange here and…'

Becky was surprised to see the Frenchwoman that Judy had described as being hard as nails, with tears rolling down her face. Instinctively, she slipped into her nurse's role. 'Oh, dear. What on earth is the matter? I hope nothing too bad has happened between you. You need to tell me everything. Why don't you start from the beginning?' she suggested kindly.

A weeping Christine slumped onto one of the settees and recounted the past few weeks to Becky. She was surprised to find out that Judy had another friend and wondered why she wouldn't have mentioned her. On the other hand, it was clear that Becky knew nothing about their plans to move to the new address.

Therefore, it would seem she wasn't a close friend. Did Judy have other secret friends?

'What do you know about Judy?' she asked the visitor. 'Did she say anything about leaving or going on holiday? It seems a bit crazy, considering we live and work together, but I know virtually nothing about her background. She never mentioned her parents or people that she had known in the past.'

But Becky looked just as stumped. 'I'm afraid I can't tell you much about family members. She never really talks about them. Estranged, I think, though I'm sure we can trace them somehow. I last saw her on her birthday. However, that was only for a short while. But I knew she was staying here for the whole holiday. I wonder ...' she paused.

'What?' shouted Christine, excited to hear any suggestions. 'What do you wonder? Do you know where she might have gone?'

'Not really, but she was quite anxious about money. She was finding it difficult to make ends meet, what with petrol for her car and everything.'

Now it was Christine's turn to raise her eyebrows.

'Maybe she gave up the ghost, if you pardon the pun, and went back to her family to save money. She may have decided to bury the hatchet. Speaking of which she also told me about this house making her nervous. She seemed afraid of it, especially being here alone.'

Christine had stopped crying and was now taking a defensive tone. 'Well, we are both afraid but what can we do? There was nowhere else that we could afford. I have little money myself or I would find somewhere less haunted. And it will take me months to scrape together another deposit. How do you think I feel being here alone most of the time?'

Becky laughed loudly. 'You are not serious about it being haunted, are you? You probably scared each other half to death with your stories.'

'You don't understand. We have both heard things at the same time,' Christine insisted. 'Banging and footsteps. And it's not always sounds. It's feelings too. A feeling of something bad.'

Becky rolled her eyes. 'In old houses such as these you will often hear noises that are unfamiliar. All around us walls are crumbling, and joists are shrinking, not to mention the old pipes. I'm not surprised you feel unwelcome. But you can't blame everything on the house. From what I've seen so far there's been little attempt on your part to make it a home. There are no pictures or photographs, no cushions, candles. Nothing to make it your own. No wonder you do not feel settled here and are not happy.'

Christine frowned. That was what their last landlord had said to them. Maybe Becky was right, and they should make more effort to appreciate the house. After all, it was cheap, and they didn't have to sign a contract.'

'I tell you what,' Becky announced suddenly, 'I've got a few things I was going to throw out, but I'll nip back and get them. If I can stay the night here, we can blitz the house and finally give it some semblance of homeliness. And hopefully Judy will show up. What do you say?'

Of course, Christine said yes. She was still dreading that night, despite the other woman's quite reasonable explanation of the hitherto unexplained goings-on. Before that moment she couldn't imagine welcoming a stranger into her house without a second thought. But at least Becky was a living person.

Several hours later Becky had completed her attempt to refurbish the house into a home and both women were exhausted. There was now a rug on the cold, hard floor in the hall along with a picture to detract from the bare white walls. In the sitting room she had stacked up a pile of paperback books that looked as though they had come from a second-hand shop. As there was no bookcase the books were on the floor, leaning against the wall. Christine was not sure about the effectiveness of Becky's makeover, but she was glad of her company all the same.

They decided to reward themselves by going to the pub where they could further bond under alcohol. Afterward, they called at the Chinese takeaway for chips and curry sauce, Christine being careful to pay her way. Once back at the house, Christine told Becky about the death certificate and how she took that to mean Judy had not intended to move out so early.

'Whose death certificate do you think it is?' Becky asked, while looking confused. 'I don't remember her mentioning anyone of that name. In fact, she seemed to have no interest in her close family, let alone her ancestors.'

'That's the funny thing,' Christine said. 'It belongs to the grandmother or aunt of Russell, the boy who lived here before and collects the rent. He didn't tell us he was related to the landlord while he was living here. When I showed him the certificate, though, he told me then.'

'What did he think of Judy ordering it? He must have thought that was strange. Do you think she told him she was doing it?' Becky asked.

'No. She definitely didn't because he knew nothing about it. At least that's what he told me,' Christine said, 'He wasn't even interested enough to want the death certificate. He told me to throw it away.'

Becky laughed. 'Typical student. All they are interested in is themselves. We should keep it safe for when Judy gets back. She must have had a reason to send for it, however crazy that reason was.'

The next morning Christine was showered and dressed before Becky had even got out of bed. Anxious to leave in time to catch an early bus, she knocked on the bedroom door then opened it as loudly as she could.

'I made you a cup of tea. How did you sleep?'

Becky raised her head slowly as if disorientated then clambered out of bed. 'Not too well. The bed is surprisingly comfortable but the next-door neighbour's baby seemed to cry for the whole of the night. I just wanted to shout through the chimney 'see to your bloody baby'. Anyway, can I use your phone? I need to ring work.' She held out her hand for the mug of tea only to see Christine looking pale and serious.

'There are no neighbours,' she said, 'not on either side of the house.'

Becky stared back open-mouthed. 'But I could hear it crying. The cries were coming through the chimney for hours. It must be squatters or something.'

'With a baby?'

'Maybe they had a tape of a baby crying. Well, something was making that noise and it wasn't my imagination.'

Christine could feel her heart sinking once again. The suggestion that somebody had been playing a tape of a crying baby was as absurd as any superstition. Judy had said that she heard a baby crying one night but Christine had never heard it. If Becky's cushions and pictures had done anything to give the house a warmer feel, her story about the baby crying had just thrown cold water over it.

'Oh well,' she said as politely as she could, 'I must leave for work soon. I don't have a car, so I have to catch the bus.'

'If you hang on five minutes, I'll give you a lift,' Becky said. 'I'll just get dressed and make that phone call.'

Twenty minutes later Christine was waiting at the front door, nervously looking at her watch. How could Becky have expected to shower, dress, and make herself up in five minutes, she thought. Then, just as Christine had opened the door, her guest casually stopped to make her phone call.

'I'll wait outside for you.'

Finally, after a couple of minutes, Becky exited the house, shutting the door behind her. In her hand was a small card.

'I found this behind the telephone,' she announced passing the card to Christine who looked at it with a blank expression. The card read:

Geoffrey Thomas
Computer Programmer
01904 478940

'Do you know who that is?'

'I have no idea,' Christine replied. 'It wasn't there before I went to France as I telephoned for a taxi that night. It must belong to Russell as no one else has been in the house.'

'Why don't we ring the number?' Becky suggested excitedly. 'Maybe it's somebody Judy knows. Perhaps she called him before she left. It could be the answer to this mystery.'

'I haven't got time now,' Christine snapped. Knowing what she did about Judy, she found it unlikely she would be contacting a computer programmer. Then, realizing how rude she must have sounded, she continued more politely. 'We'll have to ring it later. Can you come around later, after five?'

'Yes, I can. But we're not ringing it later. We are ringing it now.'

Inside a semi-detached house in a suburb of London, a woman answered the telephone to hear a young woman's voice asking for her husband.

'Hello,' the caller said. 'May I speak to Geoffrey Thomas, please?'

'I'm afraid he's not here. He's at work. Can I take a message?'

'Yes, if you could. My name is Christine Soyer and I need information about my friend, Judy, who I am looking for. I'm sorry to bother you about this but I found Mr. Thomas's business card in our house and wonder if Judy contacted him for any reason. She may have been interested in buying a computer.'

If Christine had thought before she spoke, she may have considered that the woman she was speaking to was Mrs. Thomas, rather than a secretary, but it was too late to worry about that now.

'Okay, Christine. I shall give him the message when he gets back. Is there a number he can call you on?'

Christine gave the other woman her house telephone number but was worried that Geoffrey Thomas would never get it. If that woman was his wife, what would she make of her husband knowing Judy if it turned out that she wasn't a customer? It was probable that there had been some contact or why else would Christine have phoned his number. The more she thought about it, the more suspicious the whole thing probably sounded to his wife. She resigned herself to making a second attempt at contacting the mysterious Mr. Thomas as it was the only lead that they had.

Mrs. Thomas replaced the receiver and turned to her husband who had looked up at the mention of the name 'Christine', but she didn't give him the telephone number. Instead, she rolled the paper into a ball and threw it in the bin. Her husband, however, did not care as he had the number imprinted in his memory. He also remembered that Christine was Judy's housemate therefore the call must be related to Judy. Maybe he should pay her a visit.

London, 10th May 1941

It was a dark rainy evening when the doorbell rang so Bertha hurried down the hall to let her visitors inside despite her nervousness at the prospect of meeting her sister after so many years. To her surprise, she opened the door to see a man standing alone in the doorway. He resembled the man in the photograph that her sister had sent her, though older and graver looking.

'Hello, Bertha,' he said awkwardly, 'I'm James. It's nice to meet you after all these years.'

'Where is Eveline?' she asked with concern in her voice. 'Isn't she with you?'

'May I come in, Bertha, and I'll explain everything.' He tried to sound reassuring even though he was about to break her heart.

'Oh, of course, come in and get dry James. Let me take your coat.'

James had a brief look over his shoulder before he entered the house, closing the door behind him. Bertha's house was on a small terrace next to a large church. In contrast, the terraced houses opposite stretched for a hundred yards in either direction. The windows were all dark in compliance with the blackout regulations and he hoped that the view from across the road was also obscured.

In the kitchen, Bertha was placing a teapot and two cups on a tray. She wondered if she should add another cup in case Eveline turned up soon, but something told her there was no need.

'How do you take your tea?' she asked him, over her shoulder.

'Milk, two sugars please,' he answered, as he sat down at the kitchen table. 'Do you mind if I smoke Bertha?' he asked nervously.

He had already lit up his cigarette by the time she considered her answer, so she just nodded. Putting his cup and saucer in front of him she could see his hand was shaking and ash was falling on her tablecloth. She found an ashtray under the sink and placed it next to his tea and he stubbed it out long before it was finished.

Looking up at her, he swallowed some tea then gave her the shocking news. 'Eveline's missing. I haven't seen her for weeks. I don't know where she is Bertha.' There were tears in his eyes and she knew he wasn't lying.

'But what about the baby,' she said slowly, 'Did she take the baby with her?'

James squirmed in his chair while gathering the courage to tell her the rest of the news.

'The thing is, Bertha, it's not her baby. It's Dot's, our lodger. We had an affair, just for a short time, and tried to hide it but Eveline guessed the truth when Dot fell pregnant. One day she just left the flat and didn't come back. I didn't know how to tell you.'

Bertha was stunned. If she thought that her week had been a waking nightmare, it had just got so much worse. She had been desperate to see her older sister, to tell her everything that had happened, to beg for her help, to give her a chance to take care of her. What would James say, she wondered?

'Do you think she is dead, James?' she asked coldly.

'I don't know. There's been floods and bombs. She could have fallen in the river, or …'

'You should have told me,' Bertha said. 'I've been sending you money for weeks while she hasn't been there. And those last letters, they weren't written by her, were they?'

James was starting to regret his decision to come down to London. He should have confessed by letter. It would have been much easier than this, he thought. And now he might be in trouble with the police for not reporting her disappearance. What if they suspected him of foul play? What if Bertha suspected him?

Bertha was holding her cup in both hands, as if she were holding a magic lamp, wishing for something impossible. What she said next made James wonder if he had fallen into some strange otherworld.

'I need your help James,' she said firmly. 'Something terrible has happened to me and I can't deal with it on my own. I will make it worth your while. My sister is the sole beneficiary in my will with the proviso that it goes to my husband's cousins if she predeceases you. If you do this for me, I shall remove that proviso. Eveline would want you to help me, I know she would.'

Chapter Twenty-five

It was later that day, and the two women were once again debating what to do with the mysterious number.

'We'll just have to ring Geoffrey again,' Becky said, 'and this time if his wife answers, hang up.'

'And how is that going to look,' Christine responded to the veiled criticism. 'If she was suspicious before, what will she think when the phone goes dead each time she answers it?'

'I suppose you are right,' Becky agreed. 'We'll have to try and speak to him before he gets home so we need to find his address. I suppose there will be ten times the number of people called Thomas in the phone book as there are Lloyd, but it gives us a chance of finding his address. Hang on. What am I talking about? We have his phone number. We just need to look for it against all the G Thomas's that are listed. Let's hope he is not X directory.'

Finding out where he lived was easier than expected because Geoff's address was next to his phone number in the telephone directory – with an asterisk drawn next to it. Had Judy done that? Or could it have been Russell or Tess? Someone in the house had been looking for Geoff Thomas's address, as his phone number was already on the card. It was in a different part of the city where there were a lot of new estates and there was an old A-Z in the living room, so there was nothing to stop them finding Geoff.

The two women were sitting in Becky's car which was parked a few doors down from Geoff Thomas' house. The relevant page of the A to Z was already turned down at the corner which confirmed their assumption that someone else had intended to visit Geoff Thomas. From where they were parked, they could watch the house without the occupants seeing them. It was about five o'clock in the evening and there was no car on the drive which pointed to Geoff still being at work, or on his way home.

They had been there an hour and were conscious that the neighbours might have noticed them but there was little they could do about that. Then a car pulled into the estate and began slowing down as it reached them.

Christine jumped out of the car and walked towards the driveway into which the car had driven and, as the man opened the passenger door, she called out to him. 'Excuse me. Are you Geoffrey Thomas?'

He turned towards her with a confused look on his face. He had no idea who the woman approaching him was and she was speaking quietly as though she did not want anyone else to hear. He walked closer to her and nodded his head.

'My name is Christine. I am a friend of Judy's. She is missing, and I think she may have spoken to you by telephone recently. Do you remember speaking to her? It is really important.'

'What do you mean she is missing? Why are you asking me?'

'She had your card and had marked your address in the telephone directory.' Christine didn't know for certain that it was Judy who had tried to contact him, and she didn't mention that fact, not giving him the option of denying any knowledge of her. Her strategy appeared to work.

Geoff looked startled and glanced towards the window of his house before saying, 'I can't talk now. I'll come to your house at eight o'clock tomorrow morning.' And then he rushed into his house without looking back.

Becky watched Christine as she walked slowly back to the car and assumed that it had been a useless venture, so she started the engine. 'What did he say?'

'Nothing about Judy but I think he knows her. He was acting very suspiciously as if he were afraid his wife would see me.'

'Is that it? Surely he must have said if it was Judy who had his card.'

'He didn't have to. Anyway, he's coming to the house tomorrow morning.'

'Wow! That's a result. What time is he coming?'

'Eight o'clock but I didn't tell him where I live, and he didn't ask me.'

Becky stared wide-eyed at Christine, both women realizing the significance of that last observation – Geoff had already been to the house.

On the drive back to Market Road, Christine was starting to regret her encounter with Geoff Thomas. She didn't know anything about him, yet he was coming to her house the next morning and there would be no one there but her. What if he did have something to do with Judy's disappearance? He hadn't seen Becky so he wouldn't know there was another person that knew about their meeting.

'Will you stay tonight Becky? I don't want to be alone when he comes around.' Christine's expression showed a sense of desperation and Becky hesitated before she answered.

'I'm afraid I can't because I have to work a night shift at the care home.'

'But you said you were having a couple of days off.'

There is nobody who could replace me at this short notice. You'll be alright. He doesn't know that you will be on your own. There could be a house full of people for all he knows. Just keep the front door open when he calls around and don't let him in.'

Christine did not get undressed that night. If it was necessary to leave the house at any point during the night, she wanted to be prepared. That was assuming she would be able to. She wasn't going to sleep in her own bedroom as there was no escape out of the window – it was too high up. She thought about staying up all night in the sitting room but what if she fell asleep and didn't hear an intruder.

Then her mind turned to the upstairs front bedroom. Its windows were nearer to the ground than those at the back of the house due to them being lower down the wall, and she could push something in front of the door to stop anyone opening it. She remembered Judy saying something about the room being creepy but at that point in time Christine was more worried about the living than the dead.

Opening the door, she was surprised to see how bright the room was, even though the night sky had been dark for several hours. She put on the light and checked out the room to see what she could do to make it more secure. The two large wardrobes were empty but looked heavy all the same and would be awkward to shift around. She decided she would move the bed to the door as any force against it would surely wake her up. As the bed was already near the door it wouldn't take much effort to move it to the appropriate spot, so she could leave it until it was time to go to bed. Intending to make herself a chamomile tea, Christine began to leave the room but was stopped by a sound coming from one of the wardrobes. It sounded like scratching.

She remembered what Russell had told her about mice and it put a different complexion on the merits of sleeping in that room. She walked over to the wardrobe from which she thought the sound had probably come and leant against it from one side, but it did not budge. Next, she tried easing it forward from the front, one side at a time. That too was unsuccessful. She wondered why it was so heavy seeing as it was empty, and it didn't appear to be fixed to the floor.

203

Then she noticed that the carpet did not reach the wall that the wardrobe stood against, thus was not fitted. If she could pull the carpet from under the wardrobe, it should be easier to slide the wardrobe over the floorboards. First, she needed to push the bed out of the way to be able to get a firm hold of the carpet from underneath. Once that was done, she lifted the edge of the carpet that had been under the bed and was met by a cloud of dust that attacked her eyes, nose, and mouth all at once. Russell and Tess had clearly not bothered to brush or hoover it while they had been staying in there. Yelling, she dropped the carpet and tried in vain to wipe the dust out of her mouth. She rushed to the bathroom and washed her face and hands until she felt sufficiently cleansed, then returned to the bedroom. The carpet had fallen back down but not completely; it was still bent over in the corner. Strange, she thought, as she didn't remember lifting it up there, but she put that thought to the back of her mind.

Once again she grabbed the carpet and, this time facing the other way, pulled it back as far as it would go, then tried to pull it from under the wardrobe. Suddenly, the scratching started again, however this time it was near the bedroom door.

She looked over at the uncovered floorboards and noticed a dark stain that covered about a metre square. It didn't look like part of the grain of the wood as it covered several floorboards while keeping its shape. Was that where the scratching sound was coming from? She placed her ear against one of the gaps between the old wooden boards, but the scratching had stopped. Squinting her eyes, she noticed something glinting just beneath the surface and she got a wire coat hanger from her bedroom.

There was just enough room between the two boards to lower the hanger through the gap. After several unsuccessful attempts, the hook of the hanger reappeared with a narrow gold band wrapped around it. It was a wedding ring. On closer examination, she saw three tiny diamonds set in the ring, and an inscription on the inside of it, though it was too small to read without a magnifying glass.

Christine knew she should tell Russell about the ring as it might belong to him or Tess being as they had the room recently, yet there was something old-fashioned about it and so she couldn't picture Tess wearing it. Something told her to hold onto it for a while, at least until she found Judy, and then she would tell Russell.

Bertha told James about how Susan had bled to death during a botched abortion and how she had to get rid of her body or she would go to prison, or maybe worse. James could not believe what he was hearing, and, for a few minutes, he considered going to the police himself as it was too much for him to deal with. He thought of the irony of his and Eveline's continual heartbreak over her many miscarriages while her sister was willingly snuffing the life out of the unborn. Yet, Bertha was right. Eveline would want him to help her, and it was the least he could do after hurting her so much.

'Where is she?' he asked solemnly.

'Upstairs, but you will have to bury her in the garden. You will find a spade against the wall. There are a few things I need to do upstairs.' She left the kitchen calmly and walked up the stairs to continue cleaning up. he stopped as she passed the front room. 'And there's a bicycle in here. Put it in the Anderson shelter for now.'

Then the air raid siren sounded.

In the darkness, he could see the arched corrugated iron shape of the bomb shelter in Bertha's back garden. He could hear the panicked voices of people in the near distance and assumed they were running to a communal shelter. He ran back inside and opened the front room door. Peering through a gap in the heavy blackout curtains he saw the panic outside. People were running in the same direction, away from the street. He waited until there was no one left, and the street was deserted before he made his next move.

The bike was leaning against the piano, a handbag resting in a little basket at the front. Stepping outside into the yard, he kept as close to the ground as possible in case the neighbours also had their own shelters in their gardens. The rays of light coming from the artillery guns lit up his path to the shelter which stood at the far end of the back garden. Taking a deep breath, he opened the door and rolled the bike down the wooden steps until he stood on the concrete floor. It was too dark to see anything, but he could feel that the floor was waterlogged. Outside the humming noise of planes was getting louder and louder and he knew he would have to remain in the shelter until the raid was over.

When his eyes became more accustomed to the near darkness, he looked around him, seeing the outline of two bunk beds, a table, and some pots. Suddenly he heard the humming sound stop followed by the unmistakable screaming of a bomb falling from the sky. He held his breath, his heart pounding so hard he could hear it in the silence. Then, the sky outside was ablaze with fire which was close enough to send a shaft of light through a gap in the wall. Climbing out of the shelter he looked around for the spade and found it near the wall, as Bertha had said. He rushed around the back and began digging frantically into the soft mud until he had dug deep enough to bury a body sufficiently. Then he went back inside and climbed the stairs to join Bertha in the upstairs bedroom.

Chapter Twenty-six

Geoff did not come to the house the next morning, but Christine was relieved as she didn't want to face him alone. As she walked to the bus stop, she glanced around nervously at the passers-by in the knowledge that she had no idea what his wife looked like. Presumably, she was the reason he had been so shifty in his driveway. Was Judy really having an affair with a married man, she wondered? Typical of her to be in an unconventional relationship. There was the sound of a horn and, turning around she saw Becky steering her car across the road and pulling up beside her.

'I got here as fast as I could. What happened?' she asked, bleary-eyed, through the wound-down window.

'He didn't show up,' Christine answered in a way that suggested she was disappointed. 'Can you give me a lift to college? I'm late because I stayed longer, just in case he turned up,' she lied. She noticed the other woman raised her eyebrows but didn't care.

If Becky doubted Christine's honesty, she let it go and said 'OK. Jump in. We need to plan our next move.'

During the twenty-minute drive, the two women debated the merits of revisiting the police station with the extra information about Geoff Thomas. There was also the mystery of the death certificate and the ring, but neither could see how they could possibly be connected to Judy's disappearance. Geoff Thomas was still their only real lead. As they pulled into the college's tiny car park, Reuben was just leaving the staff entrance. Christine called out to him, and he strolled over to the car.

'Hi, Reuben. Where are you going? It's only half-past nine,' Christine asked curiously.

'I ran out of petrol on the way to college this morning and had to leave my car about a mile away. I've got a free hour so I'm walking to the station to get some petrol in a can.' He looked as grumpy as he sounded.

'Do you need a lift?' Becky's voice made both Christine and Reuben jump.

'Are you sure? It would save me a lot of time if you could just drop me at the petrol station,' Reuben replied. It was the first time Christine had seen him smile.

'Nonsense. I'll take you back to your car too. I've just finished my shift so I can spare an hour before I go home and get some kip.' She was speaking to Reuben as if Christine wasn't sitting in their way.

Christine was astonished at Becky's confidence. She did not sound like someone who had never met Reuben before. As soon as Christine had climbed out of the passenger seat Reuben replaced her and the two people yet to be introduced, drove away.

Reuben didn't speak to Christine when he returned to college later that morning, so she was surprised to see him turn up at her front door in the evening.

'Is Becky here?' he asked awkwardly while staring at the keys in his hand. He resembled a child who had called to ask if his friend could come out to play.

Christine wanted to ask him why he had come to her house looking for a woman who didn't live there. Instead, she just answered, 'No, Reuben, she isn't.'

The young man began muttering something which Christine wasn't sure if directed at her or to himself. She asked him if he wanted to come in as he was clearly struggling to communicate his reasons for calling while standing on the doorstep. For a few seconds she thought he was going to refuse, however, he finally stepped forward albeit with apparent uncertainty.

'Why did you think Becky would be here?' she asked him eventually.

'We arranged to meet here at six o'clock,' he answered as if it were obvious. 'Becky thought it would be a good idea to meet up and discuss what might have happened to Judy. We are all worried about her after all.'

'Yes, that makes perfect sense,' she replied, wondering why he hadn't mentioned it at work earlier. Had he met Becky since then? Although Becky had been so forward earlier it wouldn't be surprising if she had arranged the meeting during the short distance to the petrol station.

It wasn't long before Becky turned up much to the relief of Reuben who visibly relaxed on hearing the knock at the front door. Christine wondered why he was so nervous considering he'd been there before, at his own invitation. He was acting as though Christine was the stranger, not Becky.

Becky had brought with her several large pieces of paper rolled up, along with some permanent markers. Christine feared they were about to do a group activity and groaned. Why couldn't she just take notes in a notebook? Handing out an A3 sheet to the other two, Becky told them to write anything they could remember about Judy and what she had told them leading up to the Christmas holidays. Becky stopped writing first, followed closely by Reuben but both had to wait for Christine who had nearly filled her piece of paper.

'You don't have to write what we all already know,' Becky told her which only made Christine take longer to finish.

Finally, they swapped sheets of paper until they had each read all three. Becky's contained only four sentences listed in bullet points:

- She was frightened of the house as she believed it could be haunted.

- She was going to look out the back for the first time.
- She mentioned her birthday as it was a big one.
- She rang me one night to go out, but I was busy, so she called at the care home for an hour for a cup of tea and her birthday present.

Christine winced at the last phrase Becky had written. Did she know that Christine had forgotten about Judy's birthday?

Reuben had not used bullet point but instead had written a confusing paragraph:

She was frightened of the house and had started hearing sounds as soon as the other tenants had moved out. She had found an old photo of a woman from Scotland. She said that the tenant acting as landlord was usually stoned. She had fallen out with Christine.

Christine's list was numbered:

1. She changed her mind about moving into the front bedroom after she viewed it alone. She thought it didn't want her in there.
2. We both felt a chill in the attic room on the day we viewed the house.
3. Russell and Tess said the landlord was worried about squatters and that was why he didn't charge too much rent.
4. She said she had heard a baby crying and other sounds in her room and the air had been icy.
5. I tried to invite her to come out with me for her birthday, but she wasn't in. I left her a note, but she never mentioned it. I don't know if she ever read it.
6. She didn't seem to like my boyfriend, Gary. She gave him a lift back from town, but he told me she wasn't happy about it.
7. I came home one morning to find two wine glasses. She told me her car had been broken into and a man had given her a lift back, so she invited him in.

8. She rang me in France to give me the address of our new house. She seemed perfectly happy then.
9. She had sent for a death certificate for a woman by the name of Bertha Lloyd, who turns out to be Russell's great aunt.
10. She left her driving glasses here.
11. I found a gold wedding ring in the bedroom upstairs. It looks valuable.

Becky had deliberately left out what she knew about Judy and Gary even though it might well be important. If they went to the police, she would of course mention it. Reuben also left out something - his visit to the house - as he didn't want Becky getting the wrong idea. He was sure that Judy hadn't told the others about it as neither had brought it up. For her part, Christine wondered which falling out Judy had told Reuben about as there had been several. Becky was the first to comment.

'I think we can safely say that the man who gave Judy a lift could be important, but we don't know who he is.' She jotted it down in a notebook she had taken out of her bag.

'And he came in for a glass of wine,' Christine added, 'He might even have stayed the night. I didn't get a chance to ask her.'

Becky jotted down what Christine said despite knowing it was not relevant as Gary had been the wine drinker, not the mysterious driver.

'Why didn't you get a chance to ask her?' Reuben asked suspiciously, 'You lived with her. And where is this Gary guy you've mentioned? Is he still around?'

Christine noticed that Becky and Reuben were both staring at her waiting for her to answer but she didn't want to. She merely told them that they had split up before she went back to France for Christmas. Little did she realize that her unwillingness to go into detail about Gary had raised alarm bells in Becky's mind who was wondering why they had finished.

'What about the death certificate?' Christine was eager to change the subject. 'I can't see how it is important but why on earth would she send for it?'

'She was interested in the people who lived in this house years ago. She found a photograph of a woman from 1941.' Reuben didn't mention that he had seen the photograph.

Christine gasped. 'Of course, that explains it. This Bertha, the woman on the death certificate, was related to Russell, the one who collects the rent. His grandmother inherited the house from Bertha who was her sister. It passed onto the son who still owns it. He lives in Glasgow and is the actual landlord'.

'How bizarre!' Becky exclaimed. 'She never said anything to me about this. Fancy going to all that trouble when she didn't even know the family.'

'Russell seemed surprised about it when he realized. He wasn't even interested in his own family. He told me to throw the certificate away.'

'You don't think she drove up to Scotland, do you? I mean, it doesn't sound as if she was in her right mind.'

Reuben's suggestion resulted in silence, each person deep in thought. It should have been ridiculous, but they all knew Judy could be impulsive. However, Christine was less convinced than the other two.

'Don't forget that I found her driving glasses in the attic. She wouldn't drive up to Scotland without her glasses. In fact, she wouldn't drive to the end of the street without them.'

'Maybe she had a spare pair,' Reuben suggested, 'I mean, her car's gone so she must have driven it somewhere?'

'What if somebody else drove it?' Christine argued.

Christine's last remark led to an uncomfortable silence. Nobody wanted to contemplate the possibility that Judy had been abducted.

'What about the ring I found? I can't see how it could be linked but we have to consider everything.' Christine took the wedding band out of her pocket and handed it to Becky who glanced at it quickly then passed it onto Reuben.

'Where did you say you found it?' Reuben asked, showing more interest in it than Becky had shown.

'It was in one of the upstairs rooms, between the floorboards,' Christine answered still dubious about its relevance.

Then Becky cut through their thoughts with a directness that took the others by surprise.

'Christine, can I ask you a personal question?'

'What? Why do you say personal?'

'Why did you and Gary split up?'

Christine was shocked. She had been expecting a question about arguments with Judy, not about her relationship with Gary. 'I found out that he was not a good person, so I finished with him.'

'What do you mean "not a good person"?' Reuben asked critically. 'Could he be involved in this? Is he violent?'

'No. At least, I don't think he is. He told me that he carried a knife for protection because his neighbourhood was so rough.'

'A knife!' Reuben sounded horrified.

'I think we should pay him a visit,' Becky said 'and see if he knows anything. He might have seen Judy while you were away.'

'I doubt it,' Christine replied bitterly. 'He was in hospital last I heard. Someone stabbed him. He might be dead for all I know.'

'Well, it's a lead we can follow which is easier than us all driving to Scotland.'

Becky's voice was commanding, and Christine accepted that she would have to get in touch with Gary.

'I know where he lives, so we can find out how he is from his housemates. I suppose I would have heard back from the police if he were dead.'

After the others had left, Christine braced herself for the phone call she had to make. She hadn't spoken to any of Gary's housemates, and she wasn't even sure if they knew who she was. Hopefully, he would answer the phone himself. Before ringing, she gathered up the pieces of paper and pens which were strewn across the carpet. Pausing to read again the points each of them had made in the brainstorming session she couldn't help but feel something was not wrong. Something was missing. She patted the settee and carpet where they had been, but she couldn't find it. The ring had gone.

London, 10th May 1941

He froze when he saw it - a soft bundle of blankets on a mattress. It wasn't the blankets, however, that shook him to the core. It was the upturned arm that was poking out from under them. The young woman's body was still warm, and he tried to feel for a pulse, but Bertha assured him that there was not one. For a short time, the atmosphere in the room was one of respect to the recently departed person. Then Bertha knelt on the floor, lifted Susan's left hand, and removed the wedding ring from her finger. She held it out to James.

'There's no point in burying this too,' she told him.

But as she placed it in his raised palm, a scratching sound made him jump and the ring slid off and fell between the exposed bloody floorboards.

He didn't want it anyway.

Though exhausted, his adrenalin gave him the strength to carry the body down the stairs, then outside into the freshly dug grave. Another artillery firing lit up the ground for him to make out red hair poking out from the pile of sheets, and he made the sign of the cross. He shovelled back the earth, replaced the spade then returned to the house.

Bertha was back in the kitchen and stared at James when he shut the back door. They could hear bombs exploding not too far away, however, neither of them was thinking about the danger they were in by staying inside the house.

'Is it done?' she asked, without any emotion in her voice.

When he nodded, she said that he should go upstairs and have a bath. He could change into her husband's clothes until his own clothes had dried. So, James scrubbed the mud and the blood off his body while Bertha did the same with his clothes. Meanwhile, the bombs continued to drop from the sky.

Bertha finished washing James's clothes, then ironed them until they were nearly dry. He had been in the bath for nearly an hour, and she wondered if she could trust him to stay quiet. She believed that something bad had happened to Eveline, she felt it in her bones, but she didn't know if James had been responsible or not. Her sister had seemed unhappy in what was probably her last letter before the forgeries. Had she ended her own life? Bertha believed that she probably had.

Thinking it would be better for James to leave that night, she decided to give him money to get an earlier train back to Glasgow. It had been a long and difficult few hours and the last thing she wanted was to have to entertain a virtual stranger. She and her brother-in-law would never meet again after tonight. It was for the best.

She climbed the flights of stairs up to the attic room where she kept her money in case of looters. The money was in a wooden box that she kept in a space in the wall, behind a tiny door. After taking the box out she opened the lid to take some cash out noticing the little jewellery box inside. Touching her neck, she removed the pendant that Eveline had given her and put it back in the box.

After he had dressed in the clothes of his dead brother-in-law, James went downstairs to ask Bertha if he could stay the night, but she wasn't there. He walked back towards the stairs and called her name, then he heard her closing a door in the landing. Just as she appeared at the top of the stairs another bomb exploded in the distance. For a fraction of a second, there was a glint of light that had crept through the bedroom doorway, and he thought he saw a shadow next to her. But it couldn't be, could it? Although Bertha appeared to look towards it. Suddenly Bertha was no longer standing at the top of the stairs but was tumbling down them, from the top to the bottom, hitting her head on the hard-stone floor where she finally came to a stop.

James knew instantly Bertha was dead and he was now terrified he would be blamed for the two women's deaths. He grabbed his bag and made for the back door, stopping at a framed photograph of himself and Eveline. He picked it up, put it in his bag, and ran out of the back door. With the superhuman strength only fear can give, he leapt up and climbed over the back wall.

Chapter Twenty-seven

As it turned out there was no need for Christine to ring Gary because he telephoned her not long after Becky and Reuben had left.

'Can I see you?' he asked sheepishly, unsure what she did and didn't know about him.

'What about?' she replied, giving nothing away. She decided there was no need to tell him that she had been about to phone him.

'Listen, I haven't got any more change and it's important that I tell you something. Is it alright if I pop around? I won't stay long I promise.' He sounded desperate.

Although Christine needed to talk to him, she hadn't anticipated him coming to the house. 'Why do you have to come here? I could meet you somewhere tomorrow. I don't want you here Gary.'

But he didn't answer, and she realized that the call had probably ended before she finished her last sentence.

It took him only a few minutes to arrive. He must have been calling from the nearest phone box, she thought. He looked in pain as he limped through the door and the deathly pallor of his face shocked Christine as she struggled with mixed emotions of sympathy, concern, and fear.

'What happened to you, Gary?' The concern in her voice told them both that she still cared about him.

'It's a long story Chris and I won't come out of it well, but I need you to listen to me. You might be in danger.'

When Christine remained silent, too shocked to speak, Gary took his opportunity to put his case to her.

'The reason I carried a knife around with me was not that I'm violent, but I used it to break into cars. I've never used it for anything else, I swear.'

'Just breaking into cars, well that's alright then.'

'I know it's not alright, but I don't want you to think I'm a violent person because I'm not.'

'So why am I in danger? Has it got anything to do with Judy?' For the first time, Christine sounded scared. Hadn't her car been broken into?

'What? What about Judy? Is she here?'

Gary's reaction confused Christine as although he appeared flustered, his questions seemed genuine.

'No, she isn't. She's missing.'

'What do you mean she's missing?'

'When I got back from France she was gone and there's been no sign of her since.'

'She probably found somewhere else to live while you were abroad. You didn't get on that well, did you?'

'But she didn't show up at work either. I was planning on asking you if you had any idea where she went.'

'Me. How should I know?' he said, concerned about the direction of the conversation. He decided to take control of it once more. 'Has anyone strange been around here lately? Or has anyone broken in?'

'Well, a friend of Judy's turned up out of the blue, but she's been helping me search for her. I wouldn't call her strange exactly but...'

'No, I'm talking about a man of roughly our age with a London accent. You see, when I was here last, I left something here, some money, and I need to check if it is still here. I left it upstairs, in the attic.'

220

Christine was stunned. When had he gone up in the attic? She couldn't think of anyone time he'd been out of her sight, except to use the bathroom.

'Will you go up to check if it is still there? It's just I can't walk upstairs very easily, and it won't take you two minutes to look. It should be in an envelope.' He had a pleading expression on his face.

Christine's curiosity was proving stronger than her doubts about whether Gary was telling the truth. 'Where in the attic could you possibly hide anything?' she said, forgetting about the tiny door beneath the window.

Gary remembered exactly where he had hidden it and described it so well that Christine accepted that he had, at the very least, been up in the attic. She hadn't been up in the attic since the day she got back from the cottage and that was just to check Judy wasn't in there. She asked Gary to stay at the bottom of the stairs so she could talk to him while she was up there, a demand he found odd but didn't object to.

The attic room was dark, even with the light on, so Christine stood by the door for a minute while she built up the courage to enter. She considered pretending to look and not find anything as Gary wouldn't know any different. She could check properly when Becky was there and then decide whether to go to the police. Then she heard Gary's voice calling her and she gained a bit more courage to move forward.

Rushing over to the little cupboard she opened the door and pushed her hand into the dark space. There was nothing. The cupboard was empty. Someone had taken the envelope out of it.

'It's gone,' she said when she came back down the stairs. 'Whoever you stole it from has taken it back. I can't believe someone broke in here. What if he hurt Judy?'

'I don't think so. He just wanted his money back,' he said confidently.

'Oh! How can you be sure? Where did the money come from?'

221

'I broke into a car a few weeks ago and it was in the glove compartment. I left it here, but word must have got around because I guess whoever stabbed me was after it but didn't find it on me. I've been worried that he might come around here to look for it and it seems like he has. Hopefully, that will put an end to it.'

Christine looked unsure. 'I don't know, Gary. I think we should go to the police. If whoever stabbed you was in this house while Judy was alone, he could have hurt her too.'

Gary didn't want to go to the police for two reasons. Firstly, he would get into trouble for stealing, and secondly, he might have to come clean about sleeping with Judy. Either would ruin any chance he had of getting back together with Christine, so he tried to reassure her.

'I can't see it to be honest. I mean if he killed her, her body would still be here. He wouldn't hang around to clear up. Why don't we wait a few days more in case she shows up? Then, if there's still no sign of her, we'll go to the police.'

He held his breath while he waited for her to answer then, slowly, she nodded.

'Okay. But I don't want to stay here on my own while he's still about. Can I stay with you tonight?'

Her question took both of them by surprise as it certainly wasn't how she had intended their meeting to go. Christine had refused to stay at his house when things were good between them.

Gary realized that he had been given a second chance. 'Sure, but first I've got to go to the doctors to get my antibiotics. I'll only be an hour or so, but I will call back for you straight after. That'll give you a chance to get some things together.' Then he smiled softly. 'Don't worry Christine. Everything will be alright.'

At the start of her night shift, Becky made herself a strong cup of coffee. She always began by reading through the residents' notes while relaxing in the conservatory as it was usually the quietest spot in the entire building. By this time, most of the women had been settled for the night, leaving one or two at the most choosing to remain in the communal areas. As usual, Iris was sitting near the electric heater, hogging it, as some of the other residents often said.

Becky purposely sat in the coldest part of the conservatory, not wanting to relax too much. She was surprised and slightly irritated to have her routine interrupted when Iris began to speak to her.

'How is your friend, the one who came here? I thought she might have been back. It didn't seem as though she had much excitement in her life.'

'To be quite honest, Iris, I have no idea. She seems to have vanished into thin air. I haven't seen her since she came here, actually.'

'What do you mean she's vanished? You can't just say things like that and not do anything. Have you told the police? There's a man out there attacking women. Haven't you heard?'

Iris was getting anxious, so Becky decided to calm things down. 'He's been caught, Iris. A bus driver called the police when he noticed him acting suspiciously. He's been positively identified so we don't have to worry about him anymore.'

'Well, there are probably other dangerous people out there. What could have happened to her?'

'Oh, I'm sure it's nothing serious. You see, she was researching about this woman who lived in her house years ago, and we think she may have gone to Scotland to find her family.'

'Why would she go to Scotland if the woman lives in her house? It doesn't make sense. Why doesn't she just ask this woman?'

'Because the woman died in the war Iris, in 1941.'

'So why is she going to Scotland?'

Becky was wondering why she hadn't just told the elderly lady that Judy had gone home for Christmas. That would have been the end of it but now Iris was like a dog with a bone. She put down the notes she had been hoping to read in peace and resigned herself to answering endless questions.

'There really isn't any mystery, Iris. Judy is not tracing the woman; she is tracing the woman's family and her family live in Glasgow.'

'How does she know they live in Glasgow?'

'Because the landlord told her. Bertha was his grandmother's sister.'

'Whose Bertha?' The elderly woman was clearly struggling to follow the answers to her many questions.

Becky was relieved now that she could see the conversation coming to an albeit unresolved end however, that was until she started mentioning names.

'Bertha Lloyd. She's the lady who lived in Judy's house but died in 1941. She was probably killed in the Blitz.'

'I knew a girl called Bertha. Of course, it was a common name when I was a child. You don't hear it much these days.'

'Was that when you were at the orphanage Iris?' Becky asked gently.

'She had a sister called Eveline. Eveline was my friend once, that was before …' Iris's eyes had filled with tears causing Becky to move next to her and hold her wrinkled hand.

'Why are you crying, you soft thing? Why did you stop being friends with Eveline?'

'I hurt her, but I didn't mean to. It was an accident, but she was so angry with me. She went away to work. Never came back as far as I know. But I remember it as if it were yesterday. I wish I could tell her I'm sorry.'

'I'm sure things turned out fine. She couldn't have been that badly hurt if she had a job. If you like, I could make some enquiries. What was her surname?'

'She'll be long dead, my dear. Not many live to my age.'

'Well, perhaps I could trace her family.'

'No, you couldn't. I hurt her so bad that they said she would never be able to carry a child in her womb. You see, Eveline wouldn't have a family. She couldn't have children.

London, 11th May 1941

In the public shelter, the young girl was huddled close to her father who was still half asleep. It had taken one of the neighbours banging on their window to persuade her to come out from under the bed and shake her father out of his drunken slumber. A group of children were playing together at the other end of the platform, but Joan couldn't bear to leave her father's side. She could hear the sound of bombs falling as the echoes came through the lift shaft which was being used as a washroom.

The terror of the air raid had thrown irrational thoughts into her head. Her mother still hadn't come back, and she didn't know whether she should tell her father their secret. What if she came home and found they were not there, and she went away again? If she told her father about the present, it would ruin the surprise, even though she didn't know what the surprise was either. No. Her mother promised her she would come home soon, and her mother never lied.

Chapter Twenty-eight

As soon as he saw the ring, Reuben knew immediately, even before he read the inscription on the inside, the initials SMC. Although he never met his grandmother, he had seen plenty of photographs, photographs that his mother kept all over the house, as if she were still with her. His mother was watching some consumer rights programme on television, at least she was looking at the screen. Who knew where her thoughts were, probably back in May 1941, amongst the fire and explosions of that night that she had never recovered from? He walked over and kissed the top of her head, breaking into her thoughts.

'Hi sweetheart,' she said quietly, 'Have you had a good day?'

He realized she'd been at the brandy again, the only time she relaxed and forgot about him. Perhaps he shouldn't tell her yet as he'd probably have to explain it all again in the morning. However, despite her intoxicated state, she could sense her son's reticence and knew he was holding something back from her.

'Is it bad news?' she asked him, sounding resigned to hearing just that.

'I'm not sure. A friend found this in her house.' He handed her the ring.

'What is it?' she asked, unable to focus on the delicate piece of jewellery.

Then she saw the three tiny diamonds and tilted the ring to look for the engraved initials. For a moment, her face took on a wistful expression, then one of confusion. 'I don't understand, Reuben. What was it doing in your friend's house? Why did she give it to you?'

He didn't know the answer to her first question and the second, he didn't think was important. Reuben had noticed Christine was too worried about phoning her ex-boyfriend to realize that he hadn't given her back the ring before leaving, but his mother didn't need to know that.

'Did you know anyone who lived in Market Road on the way into town? It's a small row of Victorian terraced houses, most of them are empty. The ring had fallen through a gap in the floorboards in one of the bedrooms.' Reuben wasn't sure if it was worth discussing this right now as his mother's eyes had glazed over as though she had forgotten he was there. But then she spoke.

'Is that where you found it? She would have been wearing this the night she went missing - the 10th ^{of} May.' Her eyes widened as she looked up at him. 'She must have been there that night. They always said she had been caught in the bombing, but I knew they were wrong. Someone must have taken her.'

'Did you know anyone called Bertha Lloyd? We think she may have been living in the house at that time. Could grandmother have been visiting her?'

For a second his mother seemed to be trying to remember, but then she said, 'Bertha Lloyd was my piano teacher. My mother must have visited her, but I don't know why. Perhaps to pay for my lessons. What if she's still there, Reuben? We need to go and get her. She's been there such a long time. Let's bring her home.'

Reuben began to wonder if he had done the right thing by showing her the ring. Did she now hope that somehow her mother was still there, alive these last fifty-odd years? Yet he had felt something while he was in the house, something familiar. Perhaps she was still there. He sat down next to her and held her hand in his.

'Don't worry, Mum. Wherever she is, we'll find her.'

The thought of staying the night with Gary meant that Christine's main concern was now her appearance, so she decided to have a shower before he got back. Not to waste time, she shaved her legs while waiting for the dribble of water to warm up, but her hair would have to wait until the pressure built up.

A few minutes later, covered from head to toe in lather, she heard a voice calling her name. Was Gary back already? Maybe he had changed his mind about her staying with him, she thought. There was no point in calling out from the shower cubicle as he would never hear her from downstairs. He should guess that she was in the shower. But the voice called her again and this time she knew it wasn't Gary's. It sounded like Judy's. She almost fell out of the cubicle, quickly wrapped a towel around her still soapy hair, and threw on her dressing gown.

She told herself to stop thinking and just climb the stairs. As she ascended, the attic room became more and more visible, and she could see that it was open. Was that a shadow?

'Hello,' she called out hesitantly while stopping midway. 'Is that you Judy?' Silence. It wasn't Judy after all. She continued to climb each step, treading softly as if she was in any position to surprise an intruder. She saw him before he saw her, but he knew she was there.

'He didn't notice the hatch, or he would have removed them, just in case.' He turned around to face the approaching woman.

'Who are you?' Christine asked, trying not to sound nervous, but she already had an idea as she recognized his voice from a few months earlier – and his accent.

'I'm your landlord,' he replied. 'At least I was. I'm sorry but you should have let it go.' He started walking towards her.

Christine stepped backward to match his forward movement. 'Let what go? What have you done?'

'Looking at council records, contacting family and friends,' he explained, not altogether clearly.

'What are you talking about? Whose family?'

'Mine,' he answered slowly. 'Well, you found me. You have only your own meddling to blame.'

'What are you going to do?' she asked bitterly. 'What did we ever do to you?'

'Destroying my family. My father is old and frail. It would kill him to go to prison now. He never wanted to put her in the garden, but he had to.'

'Your father? I don't even know who your father is? Russell mentioned a name, but I can't remember it. Only Bertha and she is dead.'

'Don't lie. You seemed certain enough in the letter you wrote.' He almost spat the words out of his mouth as his anger was growing.

Before a confused Christine had a chance to argue, he continued, with venom in his voice. 'You see, Eveline isn't my mother. She killed herself before the end of the war. Bertha left this house to her sister in her will. But she stated that if her sister died first, it wouldn't go to my father, but Bertha's husband's family. My parents never even wanted this stinking house, but they had to keep hold of it or the truth would come out. My father lost his mind years ago and he thinks Eveline is still with him.'

'Whoever this Eveline is, people must know when she died. Why wouldn't they? They would have heard about her funeral.' Christine was playing for time in the hope something would save her. She was struggling to follow the man's wild words. But what he said next stunned her.

'There was no funeral. My mother took her identity and inherited the house.'

'But how could they get away with it? The authorities would know, surely,' she asked.

'Eveline had always been a bit of a hermit, so no one really noticed her absence. There was no census in 1941 and by 1951 the 'lodger' had left. No one knew that my mother had been their lodger.'

There was a knock at the door. The landlord instinctively turned back towards the attic window and Christine took the opportunity to spin around and run down the last few steps. It was awkward trying to run through the small, narrow door that led onto the landing. This held her back, giving him a chance to catch up and he was soon right behind her. Reaching the top of the main staircase she turned back to see him hurtling towards. Frantically, she dived into the bathroom just in time to avoid the full weight of his body pounding against her. Instead, he crashed against the landing wall, his shoulder forcing a hole through the old plywood. Slightly dazed he peered through the hole in the wall. Two eyes stared back at him. The shock caused him to step back but he was already near the edge of the landing. Suddenly he was falling back down the long staircase, finally hitting his head on the hard floor.

The knocking on the door continued.

When Gary got back to the house to find an ambulance, police cars and Reuben comforting a loosely robed Christine, he did not even try to comprehend what could have happened in the hour he had been away. He could see the paramedics had given up trying to revive the man lying on the hall floor, but were, nevertheless, going through the motions of transferring him to hospital. He turned to Reuben, also a stranger to him, and asked him what was going on, but Christine was the one who answered him.

'He killed Judy,' she said tearfully, 'just because of this damned house. He killed Judy.'

'Did he say what he'd done with her body?' one of the police officers asked Christine gently.

Without any hesitation, Christine answered with confidence, 'He said he put her in the garden. She must be in the shed.'

But, of course, it wasn't Judy who was buried beneath the shed. It was Susan, Reuben's grandmother. And it was her remains that were exhumed then reburied in the same cemetery as Bertha Lloyd. Only Reuben, his mother, and Becky were at the funeral.

Christine stopped looking for Judy and concentrated on finding a better place to live. While there was no body, there was some hope. Christine was troubled by something Stanley Preece had said while they were in the attic, "Looking at council records, contacting family and friends." It was almost as though he thought she was Judy. But that wouldn't make any sense.

There was no investigation into the possible identity fraud regarding Bertha's sister, Eveline, as all the people involved were either dead or mentally incapacitated. There was no evidence beyond the alleged confession of Stanley Preece, now also dead, that only Christine had heard. Judy remained missing.

Epilogue

Who knew there were so many stars in the sky? Or so many natural sounds? The evening walk was always magical. The mid-Wales countryside was a million miles from East London, figuratively speaking of course. It was actually only about two hundred miles, but two hundred miles of rolling lanes.

Two dogs lay sleeping in front of the log fire which Judy had finally managed to light. She would get the hang of it. After all, she had plenty of time. It would be at least a year, probably two, before she had to start earning money again. The room in the cottage was practically nothing, Nick was just pleased to have someone to keep the dogs company while he was out on his many treks.

It had been either fortune or fate that she had shared his table at the Severn Bridge service station. He had been hitchhiking and his large rucksack knocked the cups off several tables. His constant clumsiness had made her laugh and they got talking. On finding out she had nowhere in particular to go, he immediately invited her to stay at his ramshackle cottage 'in the middle of nowhere'. Deciding to take a chance she accepted his offer and gave him a lift to her next home. All she had was her old Fiesta, ten thousand pounds, and Bertha's wooden box. In the end, all she could bring herself to leave behind were those awful driving glasses.

Tearing yet another page from her notebook, she rolled it up and threw it onto the flames. Writing a letter was not as easy as writing a lesson plan, she thought. Perhaps she should have listened to Geoff and bought herself a computer. For the umpteenth time, she put pen to paper.

Dear Geoff,

Please don't mind me writing this letter. It will be the last time I contact you. I was so hurt when you acted as though I meant nothing to you. Whatever you said, I was sure what we had was more than nothing. Then I met your son. Yes, your son came to see me that very night. I had been drinking so hadn't closed the front door properly. You didn't tell me he was so unhappy; he was furious with you – and me. At first, I thought he was going to kill me. He had brought a knife with him. But I could see that all he wanted was to keep his parents together. He said his mother had agreed to go back to you, so it is right that you stay with her, for the sake of your son. She is your wife, for better or for worse.

In case you are worried about me, don't be. I have come by some money, unexpectedly, and it will keep me comfortable for a good while to come.

I shall always appreciate the help that you gave me. Nor shall I forget those wonderful days we spent together.

All the best.

Judy

Would she forget him? Probably not. Would he forget her? Perhaps he already had. Perhaps that was for the best. She crumpled up the letter and threw it onto the fire.

Printed in Great Britain
by Amazon

19456771R00132